Tonight's Features

"You're like a film that's so bad but I gotta stay 'til the end, let me tell you that it's lucky for you that we're friends…." – Pulp

And so the show goes on, friends and neighbors. wp Quigley here, back to kick off another year of *DOUBLE FEATURE* magazine. I gotta be honest with y'all; it was a complete fucking miracle we got ONE issue up and out the door, let alone an entire year of four issues PLUS a friggin' annual issue that knocked everybody's balls back to early 20th century France. Sacre bleu!

But, full transparency, then:

I knew exactly bupkis about creating, writing, and editing a magazine – let alone fucking publishing. And lemme tell ya – it was a scene, man. I didn't sleep for a couple of days over Thanksgiving 2022 as I pored over Google Slides or some other such shit to lay out the first issue. There was a LOT of learning shit on the fly, which meant making a LOT of mistakes, which meant…

…there was a lot of coming and going personnel wise. None of us, not even the so-called "seasoned" writers, had any idea what the fuck it was we were in for, least of all me; the most surprising of which was the actual personal toll it took on me.

That very first issue? I parted ways, on horrible terms, with a friend of twenty-three years in support of one of the shorts that ended up in the issue. No shit. For real. Dude said "this is one of the worst pieces of writing I've ever read in my life". It wasn't (obviously), I'd realized my friend had turned into a cantankerous asshole, and we were off to the soul carnage races.

It hasn't stopped.

But neither will I.

You see, *DOUBLE FEATURE* isn't over yet – just yet – because I'd realized that the entire first year had been dominated by horror tales. Now, again, I kinda set the tone on that one leading shit off with a tribute to fucking *Cannibal Holocaust* – of all movies – but hey. Horror puts asses in the seats.

A Word from the Projectionist

But that left whole genres as huge tracts of unclaimed and uncelebrated of the trash cinema topography basically just sitting there. Ostensibly, DOUBLE FEATURE has been a horror fiction magazine thus far, and whereas that's fantastic on its own…it's not what this magazine was intended as being. DOUBLE FEATURE is dedicated to that slice of our cinematic history that embraced multiple genres, no matter how weird or niche that might be;   had been flirted with a few stories, namely *"Gary Spivey has Foreseen This"* and *'Lipstick Atomic"*; the short *"Tomorrow"* as well.

But we never went full, well, you know the line from *"Tropic Thunder"*. This state of affairs could not be allowed to stand a second longer, which is why, despite the Pyrrihic victories the magazine has achieved and the stress and conflict and everything else I'm putting this fucking thing on my shoulders and making – no, *willing* it – to happen.

To this end, you are in the most capable directorial hands of one John A. McColley. John's published a ton of stories in magazines just like this one, and I'll be damned if I – and you – are deprived of a chance to check out his sci-fi chops within these sacred and profane pages.

John's got a novel coming out with us in February, too, dontcha' know. Check out a quick advertisement during the intermission for **"THE WEIGHT OF DARKNESS"** coming in February, right on the heels of this bad boy. Obviously, if you like what he's laying down in this 'ish, get his fucking novel.

What else…what else..what else…

Oh yeah, right. No big deal but…..

Lucienne **Michael Strong** are back out of DOUBLE FEATURE retirement to kick in a pair of short films delivering two sides of the same story! What a fucking idea. I'm psyched they've decided to kick in for this issue; but honestly, I put the full Irish/Czech charm….

A Word from the Projectionist

…machine on. In a way, I needed a bit of validation and reassurance that this movie still had something to say, places to go, and so on. Lucienne is the proverbial Qui-Gon to my Obi-Wan (that's a sci-fi metaphor *COMIN ATCHA*) and knowing both her and Michael are still casting a favorable and encouraging eye over the proceedings means the *War of the Worlds* to me (*COMIN ATCHA AGAIN*).

You likely will have noticed the 1950s aestethic of the issue – by design of course, because let's face it: those cheeseball 50s sci-fi movies were balls fucking deep. *MST3000* made its name going after this subgenre of American cinema, and smartly at that. These movies were a dime a dozen, somehow getting cheesier and more ridiculous as they went, and there was no storyline, no aliens, no scripts, or no weird science that didn't find its way into one movie or another. To not dedicate an issue to that halcyon (actual word, used in correct context, kiss my ass) era of cinema would be a CRIME. Hmmm….crime fiction…that reminds me….

Last thing, I swear: We're kicking off the celebration with contribution from a new addition to the DOUBLE FEATURE psych ward er, 'magazine staff" – Vickie Smalls leads us off with her short film ORA". After reading this piece I wasted zero fucking time including it in this issue. I, we, and eventually you will come to expect great things from her after reading, so dig in.

Alright that's it. Above all, I'd like to thank you, our readers, for making DOUBLE FEATURE the underground success its been. It's all for you, Damien.

Ah shit, I lapsed back into horror. I'll work on it.

"You are the last drink
I never should have drunk,
You are the body
Hidden in the trunk
You are the habit
I can't seem the kick
You are my secrets
On the front page every
week"– Pulp
ON WITH THE SHOW….

wp Quigley
January 2024

CHILDREN of ANGORA
dir - Vickie Smalls

CALIFORNIA, 1978

HOLLYWOOD

The sky over Cahuenga is a synthetic chemical pink tonight, the smogline bleeding into the top of the Hollywood Hills like a lipstick smear. You take a long pull from the bottle and soak it all in. You've known a lot of movie men who waxed rhapsodic over the golden hour, who'd swear up and down that four o'clock was the only time of day to shoot anything worth a damn, but this is the hour you've always liked best. The way the clouds spark up like a technicolor fever dream, the light turning everything it touches to neon– your last wife once told you that the sunsets in Los Angeles were only beautiful because they were poisonous.

"It's all the car exhaust, you know," she'd slurred, slopping gin into an already half-full glass. "It gets concentrated in the atmosphere. And when the sun hits it just right– BOOM!" She swung an arm dramatically, spilling her drink onto the laminate countertop.

"Prettiest sunset you've ever seen in your life. But it's toxic as hell."

"All the prettiest things are," you'd said.

"I keep you around, don't I?"

She laughed, and when you kissed her she tasted like Bombay Sapphire.

The sound of breaking glass snaps you out of your reverie. John's tossed a whole box of empties onto the sidewalk, where they've shattered spectacularly. Scowling, he mops his brow. "Jesus Christ," he growls, glowering at you. "How many fuckin' bottles you got in this place?"

You shrug. "I don't know. A lot." Certainly a lot more than you remember drinking, but you suppose that's a side effect of vodka in itself.

John makes a small noise of exasperation. "Yeah. A lot. Must have cost a lot, too, huh? That have anything to do with why you came up short this month?"

You wince. "I told you, I've got another script I'm working on–"

He cuts you off with a wave of his hand. "And they'll give you an advance on it as soon as you call the office, which you're gonna do any day now– you said the same thing last time. And the time before that. And you still ain't paid me a fuckin' cent of what you owe on rent." He turns and lumbers back inside. "I want you gone, Eddie. And you can take the rest of this shit with you. I ain't a goddamn garbage removal service."

From behind you, stifled laughter– you're dimly aware that you're attracting a crowd, your neighbors loitering in their doorways to watch the show unfold. You'll concede that you are making something of a spectacle of yourself: half in the bag, wearing three days'

worth of stubble and a taffeta cocktail dress as you watch your landlord empty everything you own in the world out into the street. You sigh and take another swig of Kamchatka. "It's all just raw material," you mumble. "Today's slings and arrows are tomorrow's screenplay." You picture the typewriter keys moving across a crisp blank page: a gorgeous, down-on-her luck young starlet facing an unjust eviction allows a single tear to roll down her cheek, and... you don't know what happens next. It's been months since you wrote anything more complicated than a bad check.

John reemerges in the doorframe, his arms laden with fishnets and silk slips, negligees and sweater sets. He tosses each garment one by one onto the curb, holding them at arms' length like he's afraid they might carry something contagious. "You're into some sick shit," he mutters, lip curled. A pleated pink polyester miniskirt flutters to the pavement like an oversize cherry blossom. "Shoulda known better than to rent to a washed-up homo freak." He reaches for a white angora sweater, then hesitates. "Actually," he says, "Maybe I'll pawn this. Looks expensive." He holds it aloft and waves it at you. "Nice, Eddie! Who's grandma didja rob for this one?"

Your face goes hot. That sweater was the last birthday gift Kay gave you before she left for good. The two of you used to argue over who looked better in it. She did, obviously, but she'd never let you tell her so. "No," you say thickly. "That one's mine."

John barks out a laugh. "Yours? You owe me fifteen hundred dollars. Pretty sure everything in this dump is mine."

You move as though in a daze, feeling for all the world like someone's putting one foot in front of the other for you as you make your way towards John. He doesn't move, but you can see him go pale underneath his spray-tan as you approach– you're easily a head taller than him even when you're not in heels. "No. Not everything."

He opens his mouth for a smart-assed retort, but you slap the words out before he has a chance, wrenching the sweater from his grasp. "Son-of-a-bitch," he gasps, clutching his face. "That's it. I'm calling the cops."

"Go ahead," you say –

pulling the *angora* over your shoulders. "Tell 'em to meet me at the liquor store on Highland and Franklin. They can look for the homo freak in the Ralph Lauren pumps."

You stalk off to the sound of your neighbors whooping and cheering and John cursing your entire bloodline. It's fine. Let them laugh. You've got a running tab at the store, and while you don't exactly need another drink (you're seeing double, the palm trees drifting apart and collapsing back in on themselves), you can damn well get one. And as long as you can get another drink, everything is going to work out just fine. A car full of boys in their early twenties whips past and they yell something that might have been friendly fire or might have been "faggot," and you smile and wave, giving them your best Miss America. You even blow them a little kiss that you hope they catch in the rearview.

All of this is probably a good thing, it occurs to you. A chance at a fresh start. It's about time you got out of Hollywood, anyways, moved somewhere more respectable. Maybe Burbank. You can see it now. A neat little one-bedroom off Magnolia Boulevard with a door that actually locks and a walk-in closet the size of an airliner, and you're so deep in your domestic daydream that you almost don't realize the kids have pulled the car back around until it's nearly on top of you. You have just enough time to clock the empty beer bottle flying straight at your head before it connects, and then there's a bright hot flash of pain, and then– thankfully, blissfully –nothing at all.

***

everything is bright.

Not the brightness of daylight, but a cold, clean halogen glow that paints everything it touches an unearthly blue. You groan and blink feebly into the light. The street is empty, eerily silent– strange for a Saturday night, but at least the car that threw the offending bottle is nowhere to be found. You raise a hand to your forehead, expecting to find blood, but the skin is smooth and unbroken. It's as though nothing had happened at all.

"Don't worry about that." A voice from somewhere over your shoulder, low and musical and neither exactly male or female. "The worst thing they did to you was knock your wig loose. I imagine you'll survive." Slowly, you turn to face the speaker.

There are three of them, at least six feet tall and impossibly, glamorously long-limbed. They stand shoulder-to-shoulder in the middle of the street, looking down at you expectantly. Their ice-blonde hair is impeccably waved and feathered. Their faces look like they've been carved out of marble, all queen-bitch cheekbones and pouting lips. They're clad head to toe in skintight silver chrome, but over their catsuits they wear – you can't help but notice with a thrill – calf-length dusters made out of

snow-white **angora.** They're armed, each of them sporting what looks like Buck Rogers' raygun on matching bandoliers, but you're curiously unafraid. If anything, you

feel at ease, as though you were in the presence of old friends.

The– man? woman? angel? –in the center smiles at you. "Well, come on, get up. We can't just leave this thing in neutral forever."

You haul yourself upright, wobbling slightly on your heels.

"I'm sorry, you can't leave... what?"

The one on the left laughs and points. You look up. Hovering several hundred feet above you is a giant tin pie-plate covered in hundreds of perfectly circular blue lights, rotating slowly in place as you stare slackjawed at what must be... what can only be...

"That's a fucking **space ship**," you say. They all burst into giggles in unison. "Well, obviously," the one on the right says. "Did you think we took the bus?"

The first of the trio presses a bright blue button on their raygun belt, and the base of the spacecraft slides apart. A narrow column of stairs slowly descends from the belly of the ship until it touches down on the cracked pavement of Yucca Street. The extraterrestrial gestures languidly to them.

"After you, Eddie."

When your foot touches the first step a high, clear chime like a spoon against a wineglass sounds, and the stairs begin to move on their own. As you're borne aloft into the vessel, it occurs to you that any sane person would have turned and run, but you remain beatifically calm. The pale blue glow grows brighter. . .

...near-blinding, as the stairs carry you over the threshold.

The ship's circular cabin is starkly white, every visible surface shining bright and slick as wet vinyl. A dizzying array of buttons and panels and fiendishly complicated viewscreens wraps around the length of the walls, four white leather captain's chairs standing at attention at the far end of the room. And in the dead center—however improbably—is a smart little minibar on a white formica counter. One of the extraterrestrials breezes past you and produces a highball glass. "Where are my manners? You'd like a drink, of course."

"I... sure." The other two extraterrestrials assume their seats in the cockpit and begin pushing buttons and pulling levers with brisk efficiency. "Do you mind if I ask where you three are headed to?"

"Three?" The alien pours out four fat fingers of whiskey and adds a splash of Schweppes. "I believe there are four of us. Where'd you like to go first?"

"Orion's Belt is rather nice this time of year," one of the others chimes in.
"Orion's Belt? Please," drawls the third, flipping a switch that brings the ship's engine shuddering to life. "You might as well do a lap around the rings of Saturn and call it a night. Let's do a wormhole."

"We've got plenty of time for both and then some," says the first, handing you your drink. "Come, sit. You're going to want a front-row view for takeoff."

You follow them dutifully to the cockpit and settle into the chair, crossing your legs demurely at the ankle. Your flightmates do the same. "Everyone ready?"

"Ready," say the other two in chorus. The extraterrestrial in the center seat punches a rapid-fire sequence of buttons and the dull hum of the engine builds to a steady drone. The ice cubes in your glass rattle. You try to think of what you can possibly say to make any of this seem real.

"Look, I hope this doesn't come off the wrong way, but... of all the people you could have picked up, why me? I'm... nobody."

The alien who fixed your drink smiles a perfect thousand-watt smile and touches the back of your arm. "Nobody? Hardly. If anything, we're all a little starstruck."

The engine hits a high, keening note like the wail of a theremin.

"You see, Eddie, we've always been such big fans of your work."

You nearly choke on a mouthful of your highball. "My work?" you sputter. "Nobody on my own damn planet cares about my work, never mind- I mean, how did yo even-"

They laugh musically. "Well, the how is easy enough. Every monitor on the ship is wired for cable television. Space travel would be an awful bore without it."

"Five hundred channels, baby," says the extraterrestrial at the control panel. "We caught

Plan 9 From Outer Space

on a late-night jaunt across the Andromeda Galaxy. Loved it."

"We were impressed by how true-to-life everything was, given that you'd never left Earth before," chimes in the alien to their left. The whole cabin vibrates as the ship begins to climb to the stratosphere. "Although I'm more of a Sinister Urge gal myself."

"Oh, we haven't watched that one in for-ever," says the pilot. "We'll have to track down a re-run once we're at cruising altitude."

You shake your head, smiling in spite of yourself. "You know," you say, "If you told me earlier today that I'd be on a flying saucer by happy hour, I'd have said sure, I guess anything's possible. But if you told me I'd meet someone who actually liked my movies? That, I'd have a little trouble believing."

The extraterrestrial next to you snorts. "Well, thank god we've got you off the Planet of the Phillistines, at least. Now, speaking of your movies- I hope this isn't too forward of me, but I've always wanted to try my hand at acting..."

Below you, the world recedes to a dull blue pinprick, as small and inconsequential as any other dream

1st

OUR FEATURE PRESENTATION

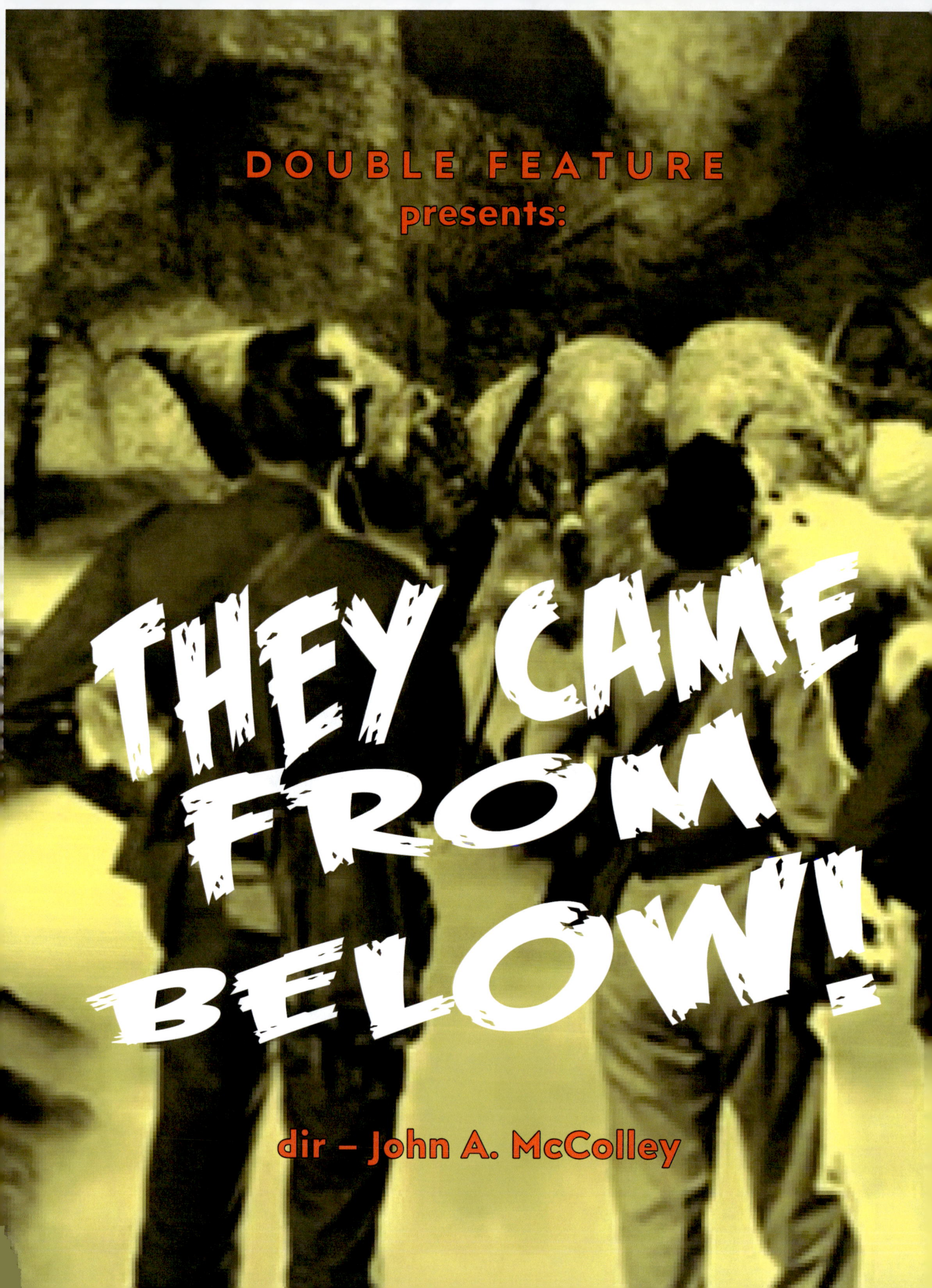

DOUBLE FEATURE
presents:
THEY CAME FROM BELOW!
dir – John A. McColley

"It's getting stronger," Carlos signed by the light of the moon angling through tall windows. Randy nodded. They both sat on their bunks in the boys' dorm of St. Francis de Sales School for the Deaf, feet flat on the concrete floor, attending the strange vibrations Cecil had pointed out to them days before and were now impossible to ignore.

The hum was more or less constant, aside from the fact that every morning and every evening, when they had time to really pay attention to it, undistracted by classes, or mealtime, it seemed just a bit... bigger.

"I think we should tell Sister Mary Elizabeth," Carlos signed.

Randy shook his head and pinched the air before him.

"Why not? Something is happening. What if it's an earthquake?"

"I don't think that's how earthquakes work. Maybe we should ask Dr. Nord. He knows about rocks and the ground and stuff."

"I read about dogs and birds freaking out just before an earthquake."

"Minutes before, just as the shaking started, but before people could notice, not days before."

"What then? I can't think of anything good making the ground shake." Before Randy could answer, the door at the end of the long room opened, light from the hallway beyond casting a distorted rectangle filled with an equally misshapen female form upon the flat, gray, floor. Both boys laid back in their beds quickly, pulling their feet up and closing their eyes. They might not be fooling anyone, but the message that they were seen was received, followed by the expectation that after lights-out conversation needed to end.

In the morning, the vibration was startlingly strong. It wasn't just growing, it was doing so more quickly than before. Even through his worn sneakers, it was clear whatever was happening wasn't just going to fade away on its own. Carlos widened his eyes meaningfully at Randy, and looked down, then back at his friend for a response. The dirty-blond-haired boy hesitated, but then nodded. Carlos imagined his own face wore a similar expression of worry to Randy's. They joined the line for breakfast, both keeping an eye out for their favorite nun.

Sister Mary Elizabeth was young, younger than Carlos' parents, anyway, where most of the nuns ranged from a little older than his Mama and Papa to rivaling his abuelitos. She was short, and smiled more than the other nuns. Some of the others attempted smiles, sometimes, but they were so unused to the friendlier expressions that the results were nearly as menacing as their glares. Carlos wondered if it hurt them to smile. It was all muscles and bones under the skin, right? Maybe those muscles were weak from disuse.

But Sister Mary Elizabeth smiled brightly at every student who came through her line, pointing to eggs or whatever she was dishing out that morning and surreptitiously signing "more" with all the fingers on both hands collected into two points tapping together. None of the other nuns would consider such requests, but somehow she always had more to give. Carlos had other signs on his mind this morning, ones like "need" and "talk" and "worry." Sister Mary Elizabeth's smile wavered with concern, but then she gave a little nod and passed him through with an acknowledging knock from her free hand. *Yes.*

The boys went to sit along on benches at tables that ran from one end of the gym-ateria to the other. Cecil and Annie, his "not girlfriend" joined them a minute later.

"You feel it, right? It's *so* much worse!" Cecil signed. "How can they not hear it? I see it shaking the hands on the clock, the leaves on the plants." The others shrugged. How were they to know? Most of them hadn't heard anything in their entire lives.

A wave of motion drew attention away from oatmeal and fruit salad. Students' hands went up for help. One of the older girls ran to Sister Mary Agnes, interrupting her discussion with the other nuns at her table to point toward something Carlos and the others at his end of their table couldn't see.

Carlos stood to get a better vantage, but there were so many students crowding around that it was useless. He climbed up onto the table itself and immediately felt a touch on his hand. He looked down, but not very far, into the faded blue eyes of Sister Mary Lucretia, who shook her head at him and pointed to the bench. He nodded and began to step down when the nun's stern eyebrows loosened and she began to sway on her feet. Carlos reached for her hand, but could only watch as she flopped against the students trying to see the first event, barely able to keep her from whacking her head on the bench. Hester ended up sitting with the ancient sister's head in her lap as she was forced back onto the seat.

Breakfast was interrupted by the older students and younger nuns carrying Sisters Mary Lucretia, Humboldt, and Steinem out to the nurse's office. Chaos reigned while the majority of the nuns were occupied, but it was mostly constrained to rampant conversation and conjecture. A few students sneaked back to the food line and helped themselves.

Just then, the high, searing, too bright to look at lights between metal supports far above faded like a sudden sunset. Over the course of seconds, they were in shadows save for a few high windows which let in beams of sunlight to strike high on the opposite wall. There was enough illumination to finish eating, but conversation was dulled. It was inconvenient, but not panic inducing. Summer in the city often saw rolling blackouts.

While breakfast concluded, Sister Mary Elizabeth came back with a flashlight, which she waved around for attention, then given to a seated pupil, aimed upward at her to convey directions by sign.

"When you are finished eating, conduct yourselves as proper ladies and gentlemen, depositing your trays as you usually do, and return to your dorms. Your teachers will have further instructions. This is unusual, but no cause for concern, and there *will* be classes, even if we have to sit by the windows or go outside for enough light to read." A surge of raised hands, palms forward and shaking, applause, ran through the collective student body. Class outside was always a welcome break from routine.

***

Daniel Nord woke with a start, sitting up in his chair, hands going to the edge of his desk, then peeling papers from his face. He'd been perplexed by a reading on his new earthquake detection system, wracking his brain into the wee hours. It was the core of his thesis, but it was giving him data that made no sense. What was wrong with the machine now? Innovation wasn't easy, he knew, but this project... He had scanned through reams of data for patterns, watching lights in other office windows across the quad go dark one by one. Dozens of sensors attached to buildings around the university all gave the same anomalous readings. There was a vibrational build up, far slower than the ramp up to a seismic event, but inexplicable as yet.

An event was imminent. Or, there was something wrong with his basic design, or a common flaw in the sensors, or his programming. But why now? He'd just gotten the last round of bugs cleared up a few weeks before. Things had been running smoothly, and he was ready to present… Or he had thought he was.

He had spent all the day before checking the sensors, their housings, the transmitters that sent the data to his computer. They all checked out. Daniel's phone rang. He fumbled for it, sleep-inhibited digits sliding the device farther across the desk before it ran into his in/out trays, allowing him to grasp the handset and bring it to his ear.

"Hlo," he said, then tried again, "Hello?"

"Mr. Nord, you sound terrible. Were you asleep?"

"No, Dr. Thewes. Wide awake and poring over paperwork," Daniel half-lied. It wasn't the phone call that had woken him. Was it? How much time had passed between waking and hearing the ring? Suddenly, he wasn't certain.

"Mm hmm," his thesis advisor intoned, unconvinced. "Yes, well, your pet project called-."

"Please don't call them that."

"Fine, St. Francis' called the main office. One would think by now they'd have your direct line."

"They do, they just refuse to use it. Something about being over-familiar with a representative of the material world. It's not like I'm a cigar-smoking casino owner or something."

"I don't need the background. It was just a comment. Call them back after class."

"Class? Class! Yes, sir!" Daniel looked up at the clock hung between the tall windows of the two hundred year old building. While the woodwork and flourishes of the window frames were elegant and still spoke of craftsmanship and wealth centuries later, the clock was a plain white face with black Roman numerals around the edge and straight sticks for hands. Insipid. Boring. Ten dollars at a chain store. Telling him he was five minutes late for teaching Dr. Thewes' Introductory Geology course. It was the slacker course of the summer session, an easy science elective to tick off boxes, but this was the midterm review before the first test. Students would likely show up.

Daniel grabbed his notes, tucking them under his arm, and made for the door. Luckily, the classroom was only on the next floor down, not far. As expected, seventeen out of the twenty students enrolled in the summer elective stood around in the granite-floored hallway.

"Sorry folks, let me get the door open and we can start." Daniel fumbled with the keys for a moment before getting the pieces of brass to mesh and grant entrance to the high-ceilinged lab. While he took his place by the massive green chalkboard, an array of diagrams already drawn every few feet and hands-on samples and equipment on display on the long workbench before it, the students filed in, getting settled at smaller workbenches. "It looks like we're missing a few people, but I think we've given them enough time to show," he said, playing off his own tardiness, "Now this first test, effectively the midterm, will cover the first seven chapters of the text plus all the labs and the field trip we took to the quarry on Friday. Yes, Paula?" Daniel asked, catching a raised hand. "When will we know how we did on the first paper?"

"I will aim to finish the grading the papers during the exam. No point in my sitting up here twiddling my thumbs while you're all working hard, eh?" This got a few half-effort laughs. Nobody took this course seriously, and by extension, Daniel couldn't help feel that no one took *him* seriously. Turning to the first of the diagrams, he picked up a rounded pointer stick about the width of his little finger and three or so feet long. "Of course you all remember this image. We've looked at it every day. The layers of the Earth…"

The inch-thick stack of notes he'd brought stood on the tabletop, slowly by slowly sliding to the left, the top pages seeming to move faster than those lower down. He moved a fist of granite from the display to the notes to keep them from wandering away. Odd, though… He kept up the spiel he'd given the last three summers, preparing the students for Dr. Thewes' exam, moving to the next diagram.

Carlos and Cecil had first period together, math. Normally, one or the other would be daydreaming about going to the beach or camping, or whatever the kids in schools that let out for the summer got to do on days like this. Today, though, both boys were concerned with the growing anomaly from below and how it might have precipitated the collapse of three older nuns and complaints of vertigo from a handful of others.

"I'm not feeling that well myself," Cecil admitted. He had been the first to sense the difference in how the floor felt beneath his feet, though he couldn't really describe it, and everyone else thought it was some kind of game they didn't understand. But it hadn't been a game, just a "keen mind" as Sister Mary

Elizabeth claimed of many of them, but most often Cecil.

"Do you need the nurse?" Carlos asked.

"I don't know what's she'd do. I doubt she has a stock of sea sickness pills. Besides, she's got her hands full with fainting nuns."

"Something to share with the class?" Sister Mary Augustus signed from the other side of the table, some ten feet from her post at the blackboard. The boys looked up at the movement and took in her question. They both shook their heads, though Cecil looked like he immediately regretted the gesture.

"Actually," Cecil signed, "I'm feeling dizzy, sick. I might throw up."

"Sister Mary Hazel is very busy today," Sister Mary Augustus pointed out.

"Yes, Sister," Cecil signed, nodding, then frantically cupping his hand before his mouth as the movement turned his stomach.

"All right, go! Go, before you make a mess on my floor!" Sister Mary Augustus signed quickly, backing up to her own desk. Carlos held Cecil's free hand, guiding him to the door. He looked back to see if Sister Mary Augustus would allow him to escort his friend. The nun made shooing motions with her hands.

In the hallway, Carlos noted the linoleum floor was dirty. This was unusual. The nuns spent a good chunk of their days cleaning and often used such chores as punishment. Now, the grit scratched beneath their feet, distracting from the rising hum. Had it been one of the fallen nuns' days to sweep and mop? As they made their way along the main backbone hallway of the school, though, he watched dust fall from the ceiling, plume rather gracefully, and then settle to the white squares. Looking up, he saw cracks along and across the hall ceiling. The ground shook again, another distinct rumble, blotting the worrisome tone out for a moment.

Cecil pulled at his hand, then grabbed at his wrist with his other hand. Startled, Carlos frowned, looking at his friend. Movement drew his attention as the floor before them split, a jagged panel of tiles rising and spreading like the petals of a monstrous flower. At the center of the flower, something stood black and glittering,

streaked with yellow and white and green. With a flash of panic, Carlos saw it move just slightly, enough for him to recognize a living, insectoid form, though it stood upright like a person.

Carlos turned, shooing, then pushing Cecil back the way they had come. They fled up the corridor. A wave of nervous energy ran across his back. His legs wobbled, but he pushed through, charging up the slight incline and around the corner. Cecil came right behind him, and he dragged the other boy through the first door they came to.

The classroom was dark, but Carlos dared not turn on the lights. The only clue he had to the content of the room were large tables with cabinets and drawers beneath and high stools in the lanes between. One of the science labs, or the art room, perhaps. Carlos felt so turned around, he couldn't recall what was supposed to be here. They huffed and puffed, leaning against the cool, slick, glazed bricks.

The door shook, sending vibrations through the wall and causing the poster hanging on it to flutter. The handle began to turn…

With sharp movements, Carlos pointed to the door, then the workbenches. Then he scrambled forward on hands and knees between the looming monoliths. Light blossomed into the room as the door swung open. Silhouetted against the lights stood a creature with no neck, but a wide slope of a mountain atop its shoulders, red, insect, eyes, and four segmented arms, one of which ended in a strange flared shape Carlos only realized was a device –a weapon?- as he pulled back behind the table. Blinds over windows at the far wall jumped and danced for a few seconds, letting in reflected, diffuse light, then erupted, disgorging daggers of glass and a fragmented view of the classroom windows across the courtyard. Carlos turned away, huddling against the table side and shielding himself with his arm.

Time slowed to a halt. Carlos, unable to get any input about the world beyond the damnable vibration in the floor and occasional pelting of debris, was adrift. Surely the thing would zap him out of existence any moment.

Or had it gone away? There didn't seem to be any more explosions, only the soft breeze off the ocean, round, and damp.

Come on, Carlos, it's over. You're not dead. He tried to convince himself. *What about Cecil?* another "voice" said. He almost looked up. Something nudged his shoulder. He jumped, but finally opened his eyes, casting them up toward the windows. There was nothing there. He looked down, and saw Cecil, a thin line of blood welling up on his arm and a small tear in his pale blue shirt.

"Where is it?" Carlos signed, hands shaking. Cecil shrugged. "Now we really should go to the nurse." Cecil nodded, then loosed the remains of breakfast on the floor, shards of glass like islands, catching the light in a different way to the stomach fluids. Carlos leaned away, then reached up to the black tabletop, gingerly feeling his way until he felt he could pull himself up and not cut his…

…fingers. On his feet, he offered Cecil a hand. Glass and tattered blinds lay all around. Carlos imagined a leathery tan animal with glass bones, laying dead in the desert, stretched along the wall across from the door.

At the door itself, which hung open, they moved slowly, peering around the jamb one way, then the other. Footprints in the dust led back the way they had come. Cecil caught his view and pointed the other way. He nodded. They would loop back around to the nurse's office to get Cecil patched up and warn the nuns. Something was here.

Settling back into his office, Daniel pulled the plastic ring on the face of the phone around to digit after digit, dialing St. Francis'. The busy signal played for a few flat beats like a mechanical sheep, then cut off to a recorded voice telling him the number was not in service and to stay on the line to speak with an operator. He looked at the device sitting on his desk. Another machine malfunctioning. Was he just cursed? Or was there something going on? Or was he just worn out and seeing correlation where there was just coincidence? He sighed and stood again. He'd have to go down there himself.

The day had gone from hot and sticky to hellacious. The soda he'd bought on the way out of Hamrick Hall was gone, and he was certain he'd sweated it back out into his shirt already. It didn't get any better as he was forced to an alternate route by a dangerously dipping electrical pole, already cordoned off by a police car angled across the street and awaiting workers to right it.

The oddities continued as he was diverted again by a burst water main flooding Avers Ave. with a roostertail of muddy water, then an apartment building on Reubens St. tilted worse than the Tower of Pisa, the low side having every window shattered, their glass scattered across the street.

Finally, he made it to the high, imposing, brick behemoth of a former monastery, St Francis de Sales School for the Deaf. Just before he turned the key to pull it from the ignition, a newsperson broke through the music on the radio.

"…the third bridge to collapse today. If you can, folks, stay in. If you head out, stay away from tunnels and br-."

"Seems like it's *not* just me…" Daniel said to no one.

The front door, a heavy wood affair with black wrought iron bands and a narrow window in the shape of a cross, stood like a grizzled war veteran, daring anyone to throw a shoulder at it. Daniel pulled the ancient rope, setting off a series of bells in offices above and to either side of the stone entryway. Even though half the nuns were as deaf as their students, the bells were visible in their little cubbies, and he had never had to wait long. Now, though, there was no answer. As glad as he was of the shade of the sheltered approach, after five minutes and two more attempts to summon someone to the door, Daniel sighed and stepped back out into the midday sun.

As he made his way around to the side entrance he had used once before, Daniel tried to peer into the offices and classrooms along the way. They were raised, so it was difficult to see anything, but they seemed empty to a one, until he spotted a dark form in one of the classrooms. From the shape and size, it couldn't have been one of the students, and unless the nuns had recently accepted an acolyte who could have played for the NBA, that seemed unlikely as well.

It did change things, though. Strangers in the school. His first thought was to call the police, but they seemed to have their hands full, and he didn't know where to find a phone. The school's number had been disrupted. Was this some kind of attack? A local gang taking their chance to move in on a new hideout? Or looking for a score of some kind? He could hardly imagine what. He picked up his pace, though what he could do against an unknown number of invaders, he also had no idea.

It did change things, though. Strangers in the school. His first thought was to call the police, but they seemed to have their hands full, and he didn't know where to find a phone. The school's number had been disrupted. Was this some kind of attack? A local gang taking their chance to move in on a new hideout? Or looking for a score of some kind? He could hardly imagine what. He picked up his pace, though what he could do against an unknown number of invaders, he also had no idea.

Carlos and Cecil crept along the hallway, eyes constantly moving, trying to spot intruders before they were spotted by the bizarre, terrifying, creatures.

Another section of broken tile stood just around the corner at the end of the corridor, but the coast was clear.

"Do you see it?" Cecil signed.

"No, but look," Carlos directed his friend's attention to the floor. Tracks crisscrossed through the dust. "More than one?"

Cecil shrugged. He pointed at the doors behind them, eyebrows raised. Carlos nodded. The stairs beyond led not just to the second floor of the sprawling building, but to the bell tower. They would be able to see out over the city.

The air grew warmer and warmer as they climbed, but the space around the bell itself was open, basically just a roof on four pillars. They breathed a little easier as they moved around the massive metal shape to the waist-high wall of brick.

Carlos wasn't sure what he had expected from this view, but when he saw the state of his city, he gasped. Plumes of smoke arose from half a dozen places. The water tower had toppled, landing against another of the other buildings. Phone and power poles stood at strange angles. Lights from police vehicles, ambulances, and fire engines flashed off windows and parked cars down every street he could see along.

"Man!" Carlos signed, "It's-"

"Dr. Nord," Cecil offered.

"What? No, it's the Apocalypse!"

"Yeah, maybe, but it's also Dr. Nord. I bet he came here to help."

"What are you talking about?" Carlos asked. Cecil pointed straight down. Carlos leaned over the row of bricks edging the opening. Forty or so feet below, he spotted the young man trying to open the side door. It would be locked, but *they* could open it from the inside...

Carlos looked around the space. There was nothing but a few leaves blown from nearby trees, nothing to throw down to get the man's attention. Cecil pointed at the bell. Carlos shook his head.

"We don't know how loud it will be. If we get those things chasing us before we can let him in, we may as well jump now."

Cecil made a face, but knocked his agreement, then signed, "What then?"

Carlos looked at his friend, and smiled, then laughed. He reached down and slipped one of his sneakers off. Cecil's eyes widened, then he got the joke, something they had seen in a movie together a couple of years before.

"Who throws a shoe? Honestly," Cecil signed.

Carlos nodded, then took aim at the geologist. The blue and white shoe spun down and down, but then hit the brick wall and bounced out away from the building, far over Dr. Nord's light brown hair. Carlos sighed and reached for his other shoe, but Cecil stopped him, pointing down. The shoe had landed in a bush, shaking it, managing to catch the man's attention after all. The boys waved and signed that he should go to the door. After a few attempts, the man seemed to understand. He took the sneaker and vanished behind the bulk of the building as he approached the door.

The boys turned and started sneaking back down the stairs.

After the first sighting of the invaders, Daniel had concentrated on staying close to the wall and below the windows so as not to be seen as he sought a way into the school. The brick was beginning to heat up in the sun, throwing excess heat back at him. Still, he was more worried about whatever was going on inside the building than his own dehydration.

When the shoe ricocheted off the wall and into the bush, he jumped. If he had had enough water left in his body, he might have peed himself. This day was strange and only getting stranger. Was this some new kind of earthquake? The falling poles and structures could be explained by liquefaction of the earth, especially in sandy areas, where the vibrations could leave otherwise solid ground to mimic quicksand, but it seemed sustained, without the suddenness of a standard quake. Now he hid under a much shallower alcove by the side entrance of the converted monastery, pressed against a door which hadn't had much direct sunlight yet. Still, the sun was shifting overhead and would resume baking him if the boys didn't let him in soon.

He tried to peer through the small cross-window, but couldn't see much beyond the gloom of the hallway beyond it.

Something moved in that murk. Was it the students coming to let him in? Or the other shape he had seen? He could only tell there was something at all by how it blocked out the little light coming from the classrooms through windows in their doors. He was torn between hiding around the edge of the alcove and preparing to rush whoever came to the door, if they were unfamiliar adults who clearly weren't nuns or perhaps visiting priests. Was that what he'd seen? A monk or priest come to help the nuns during the power outage? He prayed.

The door jiggled, startling him again. The dehydration was seriously messing with his concentration. Finally, the door swung inward, revealing familiar faces. "Thank you!" Daniel signed, handing over the sacrificed shoe. Entering the hallway was like having a sack thrust over his head. The close, hot, air stifled. The darkness took long moments for his eyes to adjust to, while the boys signed and signed.

"Wait," he signed back, "I'm not good at signing, and I can't see in this dark." The flurry of movement he could barely see, let alone follow, stopped as the boys waited for him. "Ok," he signed, vision clearing, "What is happening here? No one answered the door, and the phones are out."

"We saw a lot more from the something Daniel missed electric poles, the water tower, smoke..." Carlos signed. Daniel nodded.

"I saw it, too. It took a long time to drive here. Lots of detours. Do you have water? I feel like I'm dying."

"Water?" the other boy he knew less well, Cecil or Cedrick or something, signed, three fingers up in the shape of a "W" against his lips. Daniel nodded. The boys turned back toward the hallway, looking to the sides, then running across the hall, waving him to follow.

"Who are we looking out for? I saw a strange shape through a window. Big guy." Carlos shook his head at this as they all leaned against the cool hallway wall, the other boy peering around the next corner.

"Not 'who,' 'what!'"

"What does that mean?" Daniel tried to ask, but the boys were off again. They ran past a massive hole in the floor, large enough to drop a medium sized bookcase or a small desk down. Broken tile lay strewn about, giving Daniel the impression that something had thrust upward rather than simply falling into a gap caused by the separation of earth. "What was that?" He tried to ask at one turn, but then they were there, the nuns' day room, basically a teachers' lounge where the nuns could grade papers, eat in peace away from the gym-ateria, and take a break. A water cooler and a refrigerator stood to one side like old friends. Across from them stood a counter laden with toaster, other tools for making food and a metal sink. Unsure if the sink would work without power, Daniel headed straight for the water cooler.

After the three of them had gotten fluids back into their bodies, Daniel asked again, "What did you mean, not who, what?"

"The creatures," Carlos began, but then seemed uncertain how to proceed. The answer only boiled in Daniel's brain.

"They look like bug men, giant eyes, too many arms, some kind of guns. They broke all the windows in one of the classrooms." The boy pantomimed firing a gun and explosions. That couldn't be good.

"Where are the nuns?" Daniel asked. Carlos shrugged.

"A few of the older ones fainted. They were taken to the nurse. They said we'd still have classes, but we haven't seen anyone in a while."

"What about those holes in the floor?"

"That's where they come out. We saw one. It chased us."

"Wow, that must have been scary. I think we have to get to the office, find someone in charge." The boys nodded again, drinking more water. He topped off, too and they went to the door, trying to figure out if there were any intruders nearby. Daniel listened hard, but there was a distracting hum.

"Do you guys hear… Oh… never mind," he said, feeling foolish and rude for being so flustered he asked deaf kids if they could hear the tone that seemed to grow by the minute. One of the boys tapped him on the shoulder.

"We can't hear, but we feel it. It's been building up for days. It gets more and more noticeable. At first, we could feel it in our feet, through the floor, but now, if you pay attention, everything is shaking." Carlos pointed at a potted plant by the window across the room from the door. It was true. The broad, pointed leaves wavered as if in a low breeze, but the windows were closed.

Daniel wasn't sure what to do with that information, but it was certainly disturbing. Were the creatures causing the sound? Or where they being driven to the surface by it? "Office?" he finally asked. Carlos pointed to the right. Checking one last time, Daniel stepped out into the hallway and waved for the boys to follow. They passed him, taking the lead and were off on another furtive game of peek and run.

At the third turn, the ground suddenly rumbled immediately beneath Daniel's feet, lifting him a few inches from the rest of the floor before he leapt forward and caught Cecil by the shoulder. The boy spun, terror flooding across his face as he peered past Daniel, then he turned back and shoved Carlos around the next corner. The more familiar boy stopped, both feet planted, shoes squealing on the linoleum, and then tried to turn back. He looked up as he fought with Cecil, then dropped to his knees, putting his hands in the air as on a police show. A moment later, Daniel saw why.

Six hulking black forms streaked with unique dashes of white, yellow, and green, marched to the corner, one or more of their four hands each bearing a few different models of devices that all screamed "weapon" to Daniel. Some were shorter, more like pistols with a large, flared, dish with ridges and points inside. Others were more like rifles, with longer bodies and vaguely-flower-like cups stacked one inside the next, growing smaller as they marched forward from the stock.

…One held a wicked looking stick it held more like a sword, though it still had a similar look to it, of cascading bowls, overall narrower and spaced farther apart.

The sword-wielder pointed the device at them. Daniel stepped in front of the boys, one hand palm forward, calling the other not to do anything rash, and the other swept back, protectively. "Hey now, there's no need for that." The bowls along the long stick pulsated with pale light and wavered. The holder waved it at him. "What are you doing? It looks like you're using that thing, but it's not shooting out death beams or anything… unless they're slow acting death beams…" He was glad the boys were behind him and couldn't read his lips. He didn't want to put any worse ideas into their heads. He had enough bouncing around in his own for all of them.

The device-wielder waved it again, but the others stood still. They might have been carved from stone, or been part of an H. R. Giger painting. Glancing to his right, he saw a single creature had come up from the hole that had formed beneath him. Could they get past it? Probably, but with seven armed… whatever they were, what chance did they really have of making it to the next turn in the hallway? It had to be fifty feet away. He sighed, focusing back on the creature with the baton.

"Ok, let's start over. I'm Daniel. Dr. Daniel Nord, well, nearly. I'm a geologist. I study the body and bones of the Earth and all the varied rocks and minerals it produces, well, *did* produce, millions and billions of years ago, but still lie in hiding for us to find." The wand waved again, but this time, the creature holding it leaned forward slightly. It buzzed and hummed for a few seconds, watching him, and waving the stick. Finally, the sounds resolved into words.

"Billions of years. Let's start. Body and bones. Earth." The other repeated back some of the words and phrases in a wavering buzz. It pointed down with a spare limb ending in a stomach-turning cluster of curved claws.

"Ok, ok, I think we're getting somewhere. I teach some classes here and at a local college. So your people lived down there for billions of years? Let's set aside that that would make you the oldest race on the planet, older than the dinosaurs or even flowering plants, and assume you mean 'a long time' could be millions of years, tens of millions, even… Why do you come up now? Why haven't we seen you before?"

"Up now," the being responded, "up millions of years. Up tens of millions."

"You return to the surface periodically… Like cicada…" Daniel said, mind filling with spiraling thoughts of an advanced civilization coming from the ground every few centuries, or few millennia, to breed, or find food, or some other unknown reason, then vanishing without a trace again for untold generations of humanity, untold generations *before* humanity…

Something pulled on Daniel's sleeve. He turned to see the frightened boys, huddled together, shaking. His fear had mostly melted away in the face of learning about a fascinating new species. The idea of a new kind of geological event was nothing compared to a never before seen race of sapient, even technologically advanced, beings. He wasn't even a biologist, but he saw a Nobel Prize for medicine… or maybe peace, in his future, if he didn't screw this first meeting up.

He took a moment to sign that it was all right and he would tell them more when he had a chance, when the whole hallway began to vibrate more violently. He looked back over his shoulder to the cadre of cicadafolk. They had broken from their initial formation and stances to reach outward with all their limbs and spread their lower legs for better balance. They hadn't brought this tremor on. They were startled and frightened of it themselves. When the rumble passed, Daniel turned to the creature with the rod.

"What was that? The reason you're here? Are you fleeing something?"

"Up now," the other said, bobbing the device up and down rhythmically.

"Ok, so this is your time to wake up, but did you have an alarm? What *else* woke up with you?" Daniel pressed. "Are there other creatures? Other species down there? We thought you were attacking us, but you're frightened… Maybe the world has changed too much since you were last here, but I think it's something more."

"Attacking. Others. More," the creature seemed to agree.

"That's neither descriptive nor reassur…ing…" Daniel protested, but a plume of rust-colored smoke exploded from the tunnel, blotting the cicada creatures from view. The ground rumbled again. Something broke with a tremendous cracking sound, followed by the sound of rubble crashing down and cascading across the smooth flooring. Daniel flinched, then reached for the boys. Something scoured his hands, arms, and face, every place that wasn't covered by clothing. He cried out. Then it receded as quickly as it had come.

When he opened his eyes, Daniel saw nothing at first, but noticed immediately that it was quiet, still in a way that felt strange.

A dull green light like a glow in the dark plastic toy having released most of its stored energy swam into view through the gloom. It hung against a wall, lighting up a spot with irregular panels that reminded him of tectonic plates, framed in dark, irregular bands describing a rounded, vague, football-shape. The boys clamped onto his hands, as frightened as he was fascinated. He watched for another moment, eyes adjusting to the lower light. The lamp seemed to move, as if it was roaming around a designated area. As his vision cleared, he saw it had a number of segmented legs. Some kind of insect…

What also resolved from the dark were dozens of large bodies like the cicadafolk. They were clearly divided into two groups, the smaller group they had seen in the school, and a much larger group aiming their pistol-like weapons at the

…smaller group, and by reason of them being taken in the same moment, by the same means… himself, Carlos, and Cecil.

This… does not look good, Daniel thought to himself. He looked down at Carlos and Cecil, and their faces were drawn in the pale, dim light, but at least their eyes were open. He couldn't communicate with them at all if they couldn't see him.

A rising and falling trill punctuated by clicks pierced the silence. A series of lights began to glow before him, in a line that bounced up and down in a way he recognized. The speaking wand the leader of the group in the school had used to translate. He held his behind his back, allowing it to translate the other speaker's words.

"You cannot win.

The people are tired of hiding below the surface. We will rise and take our place in the sun once again."

It doesn't sound good, either, Daniel thought. Another trill.

"Walk." The smaller group began moving forward. As far as Daniel could tell, they hadn't signaled one another or discussed their next move. Perhaps they had done so before they had come to the surface. They passed another glowing insect, then another on the near wall. He spotted others, along what he figured was the opposite wall of the corridor, but they seemed far away. He wished there was more light, to be able to see the whole chamber better.

They were ushered into a smaller space, with one singular light crawling around the ceiling he gauged to be no more than ten feet away. There was a grinding sound, and the dim square of light coming from the hallway irised closed as Daniel watched.

"Well, that's great. Miles below the surface and sealed into a tomb."

"Not a tomb. Contemplation."

"'Contemplation?' That's a bigger word for you, and not one you mimicked from me," Daniel said.

"No, while most of us sleep during the down time, some guard the rest from digging animals and wake us if there's a larger problem like danger of a chamber collapsing," the leader said.

"Or insurrection?" Daniel said.

"Yes. For harvest," the other said, the words making Daniel's heart race. "When we visit the surface, it is mostly for the purposes of connecting with other hives. 'Hive' is not quite the right word, but I think the idea comes across, like 'city,' but also not quite. In addition to taking mates and producing the next generation, we explore, observe the world, and take samples for our museums and zoos."

"Samples?" Daniel asked, mind shooting to the worst case. "Is that why we're here?"

"No, we don't take intelligent species, though we haven't found many, either. We have pools of crustaceans from ages gone, lizard creatures from some eras after that… various plants and insects and mammals as they changed and grew…"

"Crustaceans from before the lizards… the dinosaurs? … like… Trilobites?" Daniel drew in the dust of the floor: the rounded front, tapered body and classic three lobes of the most populous fossils from the sea. He had always admired the vanished creatures, only found in stones' memory, but having lived for so long… but not, apparently, as long as the cicadafolk… Something occurred to him. "What do you call yourselves? We call ourselves 'humans' or 'humanity.'"

"We are familiar. And you have many groups, nations, that call themselves different things, and languages. I had to listen at the beginning, allow the device to calibrate to… English. North American. What we call ourselves doesn't translate perfectly, but those of us who have watched you have devised the name…'" But the earth shook again at that moment. The walls buckled. The light bug lost its grip on the ceiling and fell, dangling by some kind of cord, making the glow sway and spin, throwing light and shadow around like an amusement park ride. Daniel wasn't amused, though.

"…we have… diverged from the natural order, following along your peoples' progress. Many more stay awake now, perhaps unwisely so, listening to your broadcasts. It is not good to subvert one's nature in pursuit of goals beyond continuing the self and the community."

"Broadcasts? You can hear our radio and television shows?"

"Some of them. They first came to us nearly a century ago, but while they grew larger and louder for a time, they had faded recently. Some of us were concerned that there had been some calamity, others took this as a sign you were ready."

"'Ready?'" Carlos was more frightened than he could ever remember being, even when his father was sick in the hospital or he'd sneaked from the screen showing the Fun Bears movie to the one where Red Rover was already tearing into tourists, throwing blood and gore everywhere. The experience had left him uncertain when his parents offered to get him a dog later that year. Lucky was nothing like Red, and he wished the lab was here now.

Instead, Carlos clung to Cecil. He and Randy were his best friends since he was spending so much time at the school. He hoped Randy was all right. Was the school even still there? Would it be there when all this was done? What would he do? Go back home and go to school with all those hearing people again?

The light swung wildly, the creature creating it trying to climb back up its cord to the ceiling. He reached for Daniel, pulling on his arm again. "What's going on? This is scary," he signed. Daniel nodded.

"I'm sorry. I don't really know what do to, but I'll try to get you back home safe," the teacher signed. The man's hands shook. His face was drawn. Carlos nodded at him, smiling to try to show he was confident in the geologist.

Darkness consumed the meager light in a blink. Dust filled the air, Carlos' lungs. Something crashed into the floor, sending vibrations into his feet. He coughed and sputtered, reaching out around him for Cecil and Dr. Nord. He caught cloth and held on. Another hand grabbed him back, small. Cecil. An alien smell shot up his nose, stabbing, grating.

He coughed and sneezed and choked. Someone pushed him, then lifted for a moment before setting him back down unsteadily. He fell, losing his grip on Cecil, but whoever had pushed him landed over him, barely supporting itself, breathing heavily in his face.

Dawn came in another blink, blinding, lighting up swirling clouds of dust. Carlos threw a hand up before his eyes, striking the person above him. It wasn't Dr. Nord. It was one of the creatures. *One of them saved us.* He wondered, confused as he was lifted back to his feet. His eyes adjusted to the light and he saw the ceiling of the wide, low room had collapsed, forming a ramp into the space above.

A bar of light shone steadily. Black insectmen staggered toward it, shielding their own eyes. One of the creatures still on the floor stood and heaved Dr. Nord onto his shoulder, carrying him up the slope. The one before them moved to do the same, but Carlos batted the bristly, hard appendage away and started forward on his own. Cecil wove on his feet, but took his hand and they ran as best they could toward the light.

On the next floor stood a panoramic window onto a lush jungle. Insects flitted and crawled along plants Carlos had never seen before. A boulder shifted, shaking tall grasses. With a flash of realization, Carlos saw that the pale brown lump was actually a turtle. He pulled on Cecil's hand and pointed with his free one. The insectmen didn't stop to look, but ran along a curved hallway. Cecil glanced at the turtle, but then pointed after the escapees. He was right. They should probably try to keep up.

A spiderweb of cracks suddenly appeared on the window, reaching outward. The world swam a bit and Carlos' legs felt just as wobbly as they had in the school when they had seen the first insect creature. This was followed by a second expanse of cracks, but smaller this time, and lower on the window. Cecil pulled again and Carlos stumbled forward. Once he was moving, he felt his head clear, his muscles regained their strength.

Cecil tripped. He tried to catch himself and tumbled, landing flat on his back. Carlos shot a look over his shoulder. Dozens of the insectmen charged toward them, weapons bobbing in front of them as they came. One weapon jerked, but didn't shoot any kind of missile or beam Carlos could see. A blink later, the wobbliness came over him again, his right arm and shoulder feeling like jelly. Invisible beams… sound? They were attacking deaf kids with sound? He almost laughed, but then his left leg began to wobble and he sat hard on the smooth stone floor beside Cecil.

Dazed, Carlos slumped over, his body not responding at all. Fear surged through him, but there wasn't anything he could do but watch the strange subterranean world tip over on its side, a strip of prehistoric jungle visible amid the vaguely orange stone. Iron. He realized as he stared. Dr. Nord had been teaching them about rocks, and when there was orange like that, it meant rust. Not that it helped him right then.

A black form appeared above him, and he was scooped up as Dr. Nord had been. He hung, helpless, at an awkward angle as the creatures didn't have shoulders in the same way humans did, staring at a bobbing army of insectmen. There had to be hundreds now, flooding the broad hallway and firing their sound beams. Another of the creatures had grabbed Cecil. *What do they want us for?* He wondered, *and why are they shooting at their own and trapping them in rooms? Is this a war?*

They turned a corner, blocking off Carlos' view of the pursuing army, then another. A short hallway later, they passed through a much thicker section of wall. Door panels grew out of the edge of the doorway, sliding across. *Not exactly the same as the other door, but I guess we have different kinds of doors up there, too.*

Carlos was set down at the foot of a curved wall beside Cecil and Dr. Nord, both of whom were awake, but looked confused. Another insectman walked up to them while the others gathered around some large, round panels with knobs all over the slanted tops, seeming to discuss what they would do next. The lone creature before them waved its wand at him and Cecil, but it had even less effect than the guns.

"I don't know what you want," Carlos signed, "I don't understand." The creature kept trying, waving the tapered device at each of them in turn. Eventually, Dr. Nord sat up straighter. He nodded, then spoke. It was difficult to read his lips in the half-light of a dozen roaming insects around the continuous wall of the circular room. There were also a couple of insects tethered above the panels, apparently attached to some kind of pillar in the center of the room. He wondered it if was a computer or maybe the source of the hum that had traveled all the way up through the crust to the town.

Carlos sat up, startled by shaking of the wall he leaned on. Many of the insectmen turned toward the door and then back to each other. Dr. Nord struggled to his feet and came over to the boys. He crouched down and began to sign, hands shaky, imprecise. He was stilled muddled by the sound weapon.

"We weren't meant to be in the middle of this, but we are now."

"War," Carlos signed. Dr. Nord nodded.

"Yes, its looks like after decades of listening on us from down here, we've poisoned their harmony."

"What can we do?" Cecil asked.

"They're going to send us back up and destroy the elevator." Dr. Nord signed. Carlos rocked back, laughing.

"What? What's funny?" Dr. Nord looked at him as though *he* had turned into a seven foot tall insect.

"Randy just told me a joke about a bug on an elevator the other day!" Carlos managed to sign over the course of half a minute of trying to control himself. When he did, Cecil pointed, eyebrows raised in recognition and laughed as well, which set Carlos off again. After a minute Dr. Nord put a hand on each of their shoulders.

"I understand this is all very scary, and a moment of fun makes it bearable, but the fun is

"What do we do?"

"We've got to get into the… device." Dr. Nord pointed. "They'll help us strap in." He stood and waved the boys forward, following one of the insectmen to a low ramp between the panels to a door in the base of the pillar. Within, there was a round of seats against the wall and a central seat at a small console. The boys were seated along the wall. The insectman drew an appendage along the bench, toward the center of the chamber, causing bars of stone to rise from the seat and from the wall, growing around to hold the boys each firmly. The room shook. A crack appeared in outer wall of the larger room.

Dr. Nord sat at the center. When the insectman had activated his restraints, he pointed to the console, then out through the open doorway, waving the glowing stick at Dr. Nord. Dr. Nord nodded.

"Let's go!" Cecil signed. He was as ready to get home as Carlos.

"That's the tough part. We can't leave until that door opens." Dr. Nord pointed.

"Why?" Carlos asked.

"I've got to push this button."

"They can't launch us from out there? All those controls?"

"I think they… broke those controls so the others can't bring us back or stop what's happening." The room shook again. The crack in the wall became a spiderweb network of breaks. A few pieces of stone fell to the floor. Carlos could see movement beyond.

"I think we should go. Hit the button." Carlos signed, his arm motion limited by the stone restraints.

"I have to wait." Another crash. More chunks scattering across the floor. The insectmen inside the round room turned from their conversation, bringing up the few weapons they had, forming a wall at the base of the ramp.

"They're coming through."

"I know."

"We have to go!" Carlos tried, but Dr. Nord had closed his eyes and turned away. Something more was happening here. Why didn't they just leave? Dr. Nord held a shaking hand over the control the insectman had pointed out. He turned partway back to watch the doors.

The doors, which had fused on closing to look like a seamless recess in the round wall, collapsed, shards of stone flying across the room. Carlos saw a device like the sound beam pistols, but ten times, fifty times, bigger. Two insectmen stood behind the curved dish at a control panel.

Defenders fell. Fallen chunks of door slid across the floor. Dozens of black forms glinted in the half light, their weapons bobbing, catching the wall-crawling insects' light. Then it was hundreds, an uncountable roiling sea of oily waves.

"We have to-" Carlos tried to sign again, but he saw that Dr. Nord was slumped over in the control seat. He fought against the stone restraints for a few seconds, then closed his eyes, calming himself and trying to recall exactly what the insectman had done to summon the stone bars. He reached for the spot but it was too far. It would probably have been easier with another set of arms… or legs.

…insectman had done to summon the stone bars. He reached for the spot but it was too far. It would probably have been easier with another set of arms… or legs.

Legs. Carlos thought. *Maybe?* He shoved a shoe off, pushing down the heel with the toe of the other, and brought his foot up as though sitting with one foot across his lap as he had seen his father do from time to time. He drew his toes along the spot he thought the creature had slid its digits, but nothing happened. Maybe there was more to it.

He felt eyes upon him and looked up to see a trio of insectmen standing in the open doorway of the elevator. He flopped his foot more frantically. He had to push the button now! One of the insectmen fired his weapon. Carlos felt the wobbles roll through him. The room swam. His foot dragged across the stone bench, then he fell over onto his side and slid onto the floor.

Was this success? Would he be able to stand to get to the panel? Was Dr. Nord knocked out? Or something worse? All of these concerns ran through Carlos' head as he waited for the insectmen to come around the panels and kill him.

No! He yelled inside his head. If they failed to get home, these creatures would keep coming. He had seen hundreds himself. How many were there? Thousands? Millions?

Just their elevators alone could devastate any city they came up under. But what if they brought those cannons? Buildings would fall like dominoes.

He curled his hands into fists, tighter, tighter, willing his strength back. He tried to roll onto his hands and knees and barely flopped. He tried again, rolling onto his belly, but he couldn't get his legs to do anything. He reached out with his arms and pulled himself toward Dr. Nord. He grabbed the man's pant leg and pulled himself up to an unsteady kneel.

He saw one of the insectmen at the same time it saw him. With a snarl on his lips, he lunged forward, smacking the control Dr. Nord had meant to hit and the whole platform shot up, slamming into his elbow. The limb smacked into his face and he felt a crack and a sharp pain between his shoulder and elbow. Darkness closed in around him. The last thing he noticed was the hum was back, and coursing through his whole body.

**

Carlos awoke in a hospital room. Everything was shades of white and gray. For a moment he though he'd somehow gone colorblind, which was as hilarious to him as Randy's elevator bug joke and he burst out laughing, which jarred his arm and startled him out of the fit with a jolt of pain. A flutter of movement drew his attention. He looked over to see the curtain between beds being drawn back.

Cecil stood beside the other bed. Dr. Nord sat propped up, bandages over various parts of his body, but most notably his ears. He waved slowly and gave a weak smile. Bruises around his eyes made him look like a raccoon, or someone who just found out they weren't a very good boxer.

"I'm glad you're awake," Dr. Nord signed, "how do you feel?"

"Like a towel that just came out of the washing machine," Carlos said. Dr. Nord looked to Cecil, who signed something else, perhaps explaining the joke. Dr. Nord had been improving his signing, but wasn't very skilled.

"They say you broke your arm. How did you even get out of the seat?"

"With a lot of effort, and a little help from-" the moment came flooding back to Carlos. "The insectmen. There were three on the elevator."

"The government has them. I can't imagine we'll ever see them again," Dr. Nord said. That relaxed Carlos. At least the aggressive creatures weren't wandering the streets looking for buildings to fell and people to kidnap.

"How about you?" Carlos asked, "Your ears?"

"The sonic weapon they used to break down the wall," Dr. Nord got through with help from Cecil, "shattered the bones of my inner ear, as well as damaging almost every other bone in my body. The others will heal, but… I'll never hear again."

"I'm sorry," Carlos signed, his fist making circles on his chest.

"It's nothing you haven't had to deal with, but I'm not sure what it means for my career as a teacher," Dr. Nord said.

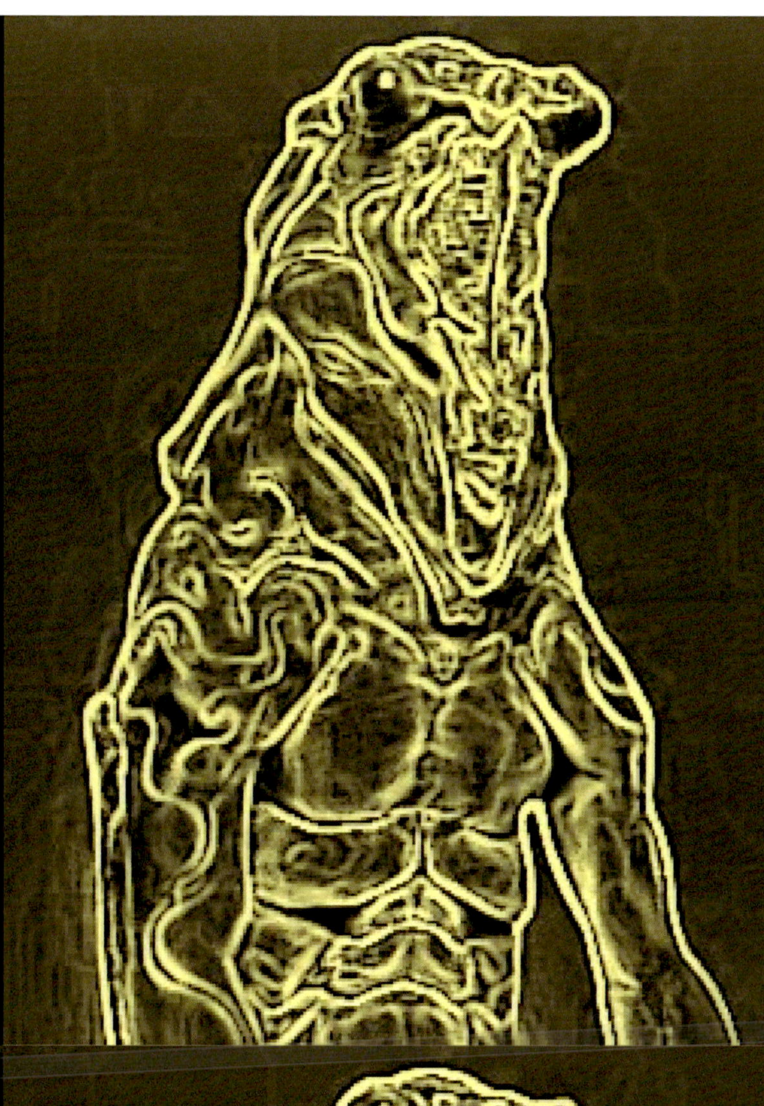

Two months later…

"If you have a question, you'll have to address it to my assistant," Dr. Nord said, pointing at the computer at the end of the workbench. He would learn how to read lips, but for now, it was the best he could do. He knew how to speak when he had lost his hearing, so he could still bore Dr. Thewes' students, even if he needed speech therapy. His signing was coming along, but now his visits to St. Francis de Sales School for the Deaf was more of a mutual learning experience.

END

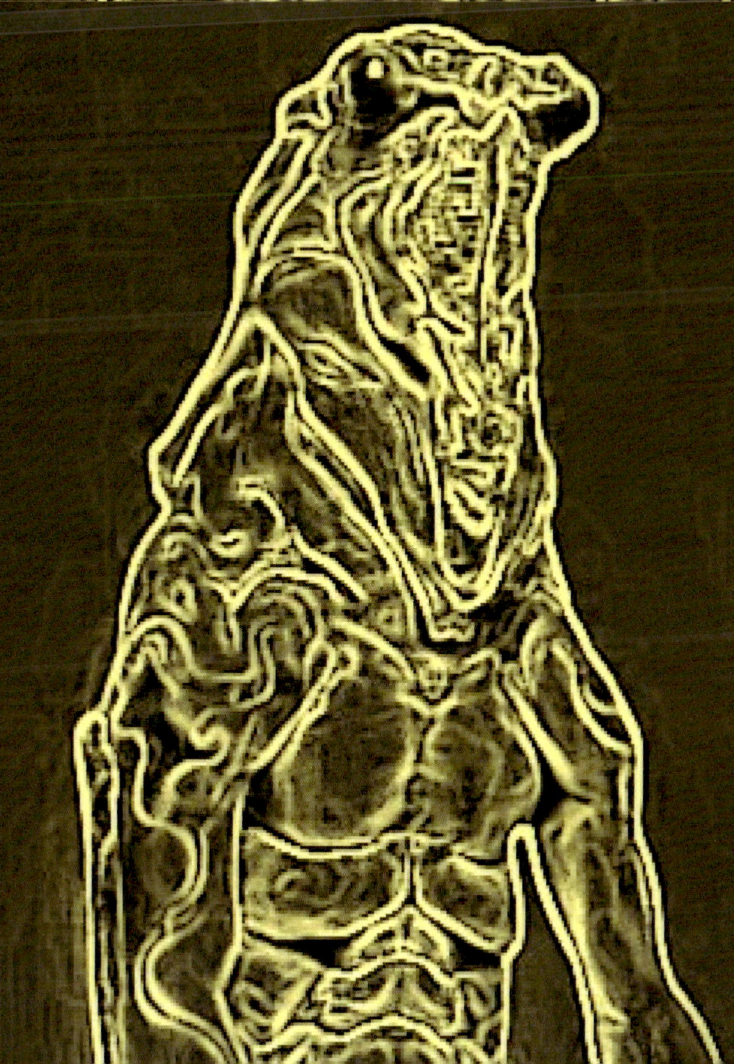

INTERMISSION

John A. McColley

THE WEIGHT OF DARKNESS

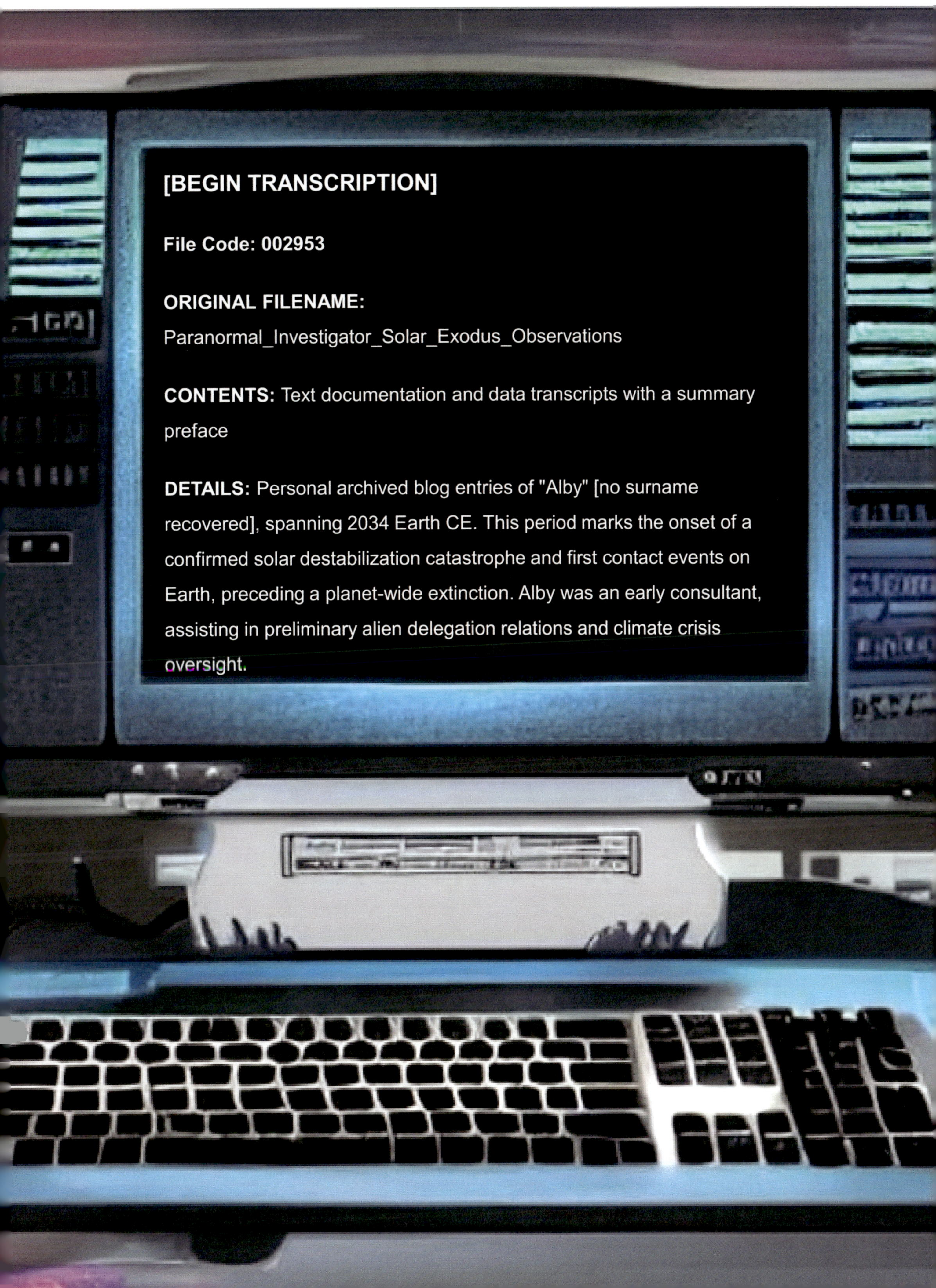

[BEGIN TRANSCRIPTION]

File Code: 002953

ORIGINAL FILENAME:

Paranormal_Investigator_Solar_Exodus_Observations

CONTENTS: Text documentation and data transcripts with a summary preface

DETAILS: Personal archived blog entries of "Alby" [no surname recovered], spanning 2034 Earth CE. This period marks the onset of a confirmed solar destabilization catastrophe and first contact events on Earth, preceding a planet-wide extinction. Alby was an early consultant, assisting in preliminary alien delegation relations and climate crisis oversight.

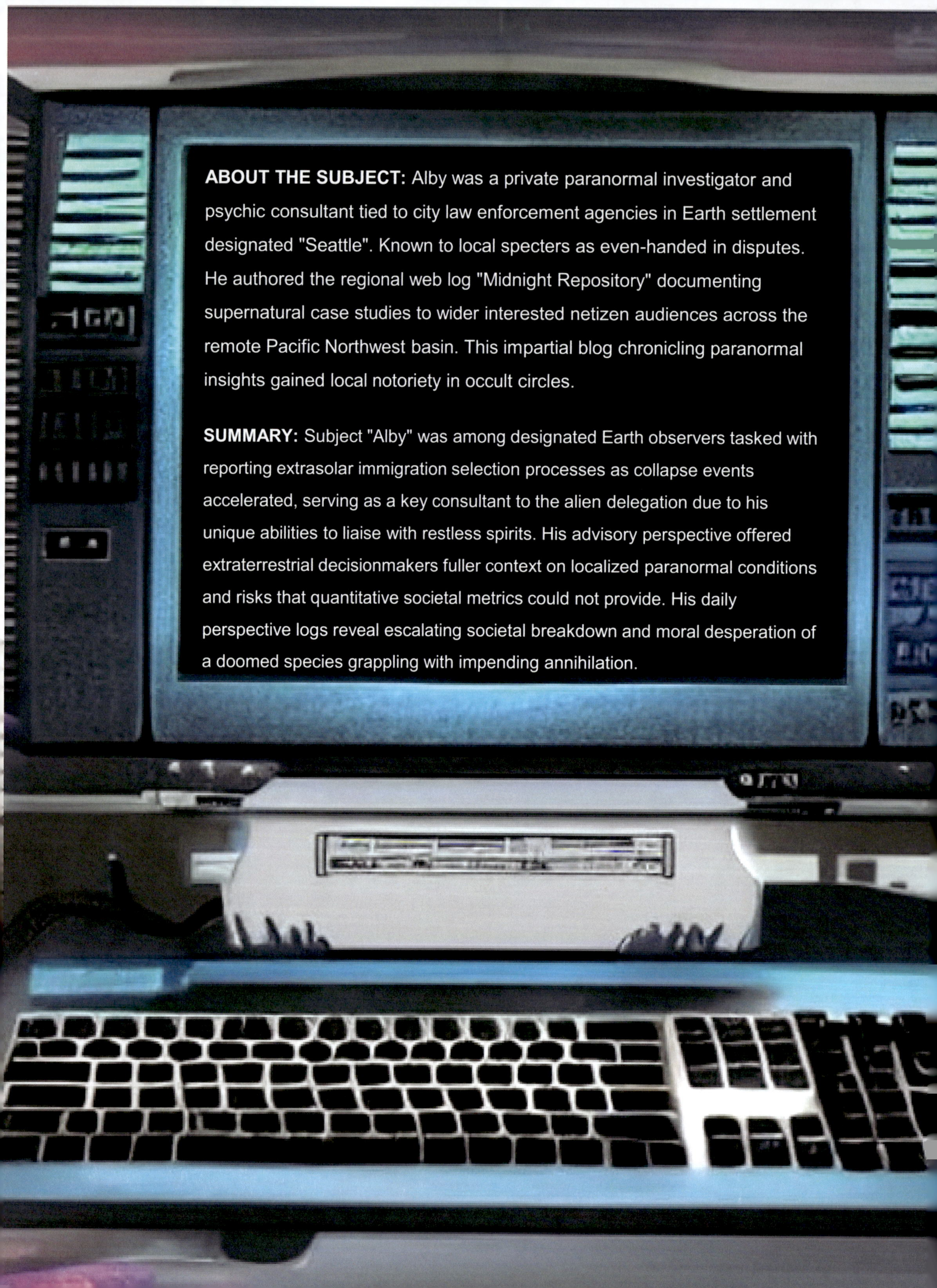

ABOUT THE SUBJECT: Alby was a private paranormal investigator and psychic consultant tied to city law enforcement agencies in Earth settlement designated "Seattle". Known to local specters as even-handed in disputes. He authored the regional web log "Midnight Repository" documenting supernatural case studies to wider interested netizen audiences across the remote Pacific Northwest basin. This impartial blog chronicling paranormal insights gained local notoriety in occult circles.

SUMMARY: Subject "Alby" was among designated Earth observers tasked with reporting extrasolar immigration selection processes as collapse events accelerated, serving as a key consultant to the alien delegation due to his unique abilities to liaise with restless spirits. His advisory perspective offered extraterrestrial decisionmakers fuller context on localized paranormal conditions and risks that quantitative societal metrics could not provide. His daily perspective logs reveal escalating societal breakdown and moral desperation of a doomed species grappling with impending annihilation.

Recovered Blog:
Midnight Repository

dir: Michael Strong

[03-15-2034] First Contact

Was focused on an older open case file, trying in vain to spot fresh connections in the underlined newspapers clippings for the dozenth time, when all the screens in the station bullpen suddenly sputtered to static. Every beat cop's smartphone, the captain's office tube TV...even te glitchy basement feed all washed over in chaotic black and white speckles mirrored on five puzzled faces. Then the wall-mounted antique set sharpened focus on some crude sputnik CGI graphic and an AMBER Alert-style framing around stark type - "Emergency Broadcast Announcement".

After strained minutes staring at that retro sci-fi reject graphite rocket while necks craned around me, a discount exec came in from the wings offering limp platitudes building up to the big reveal - "We have made off-planet contact."

Figures the trickle down of actual intel would be slower than the station's leaden coffee, but electronic murmurs confirmed this broadcast blast reached global eyeballs first.

In my mind, I was already flipping through a rolodex of faces with convenient abduction stories to anticipate alibis inundating Detective White's desks for weeks. At least this first contact edged over more destructive revelations. Though now I'll need to brace for the torrent of spirits flooding Earth's crust if interplanetary exchanges sow unrest. But I have a front row seat for the show.

[03-17-2034] Extinction Level Warnings

The second alien bulletin, another shrill emergency broadcast, carried urgent solar collapse forecasts in Earth months - "imminent gravitational failure", "conditions incompatible with carbon life". Had to tune out the recycled talking head

theories and solidify practical plans. If these clerks of superior technology predict immediate catastrophe, why wait so long to warn the belligerent ants crawling around Earth's surface? What are they really gauging by offering such sparse salvation to a speck they could crush?

Dreams are getting pushier, like they've got something to prove. There's this one phrase, keeps elbowing its way in — *'Wake up, Lisa. Wake up.'* No idea who she is. Probably some cosmic wrong number. But it's insistent, like a broken record with an attitude problem. Maybe it's a sign, or maybe the universe's spam. Who knows? But hey, if some ghostly voice wants Lisa up and at 'em, who am I to argue? Just passing along the message. Lisa, if you're out there, consider this your wake-up call.

How will society fragment when all hopes pivot on statistical death sentences and golden ticket lotteries? Those already... assembling in peaks closer to the stars harbor a darker denial, but no mass delusion will stall a dying star.

[03-19-2034] A Lifeline

Latest shocking broadcast bulletin - our new interstellar pals are extending an olive branch offer to "preserve humanity" since their advanced tech spotted signs of imminent solar failure first. After initial contact and news the sun is dying, finally things are looking up.

No doubt their motives issued from sheer boredom after monitoring Earth's crop of melodramatic programming and news cycle hysteria. We must seem like Reality TV with better CGI explosions. Still, given imminent solar demise forecasts, beggars can't be planetary choosers.

Have to wonder though what selective criteria these extraterrestrials placed on rescue candidates when scanning our networks. Doubt occult detectives and jaded loners rank high on survival asset scorecards. My background best suits assisting restless spirits across lightyears of alien afterlife bureaucracy. Here's hoping bureaucracies (and ghosts) span galaxies universally.

As one of the few experts mediating between spectral and human realms, the aliens rely on my insights to assess local environment stability as global order crumbles. If specter-wrangling skills persuade them I'm worth the fuel costs, maybe I'll luck out. The break room coffee can't be any worse on an advanced homeworld, right? Hopefully further communications elaborate how we meet criteria.

03-21-2034] Hard Proof Of Our Solar Timebomb

After enough backchannel pleas and warnings, higher-ups finally leaked raw solar analysis data the alien delegation provided our scientists. I pored over the models and inescapable projections all night - no doubt now our interstellar harbingers didn't exaggerate the solar threat.

Clear collapse trajectories based on unprecedented fusion instability measured over last year. Their superior tracking technology must employ intricate solar mesh scans and gravitational wave analysis to have detected those cascading instability indicators before our primitive terrestrial equipment. Chilling to behold that view of the dispassionate, perfect cosmic spheres spelling our system's demise.

Talk now of continent-wide extinction level events as the projection models indicate total loss of magnetic shielding and irradiation bursts within the decade. At least this early detection should allow some fractions of the population to find temporary havens as society fragments. I'll need to complete my ongoing investigations soon. Let's hope our alien correspondents share refuge specifics sooner than later while panic and unrest build.

The swelling waves of human panic breed equal dread within the spectral realm - even the restless dead grasp the cosmic finality beyond all mythical resurrections when stars expire. This new interstellar afterlife promises no familiar haunts across such unfathomable gulfs.

[03-22-2034] Bugging Out To The Stars?

Imminent solar extinction projections now populate mainstream chatter, this extraterrestrial coalition finally floated concrete moral relief - transport sanctuary to rebuild human civilization on one of their established worlds once Earth grows fully inhospitable. Vague talk of "preserving mankind's continuance".

No specifics yet what selective criteria gets applied on their manifest rocket passenger lists. But the growing Congressional fanfare and presidential proxies posing at podiums made clear governments expected some shiny salvation tickets to start trickling down soon. Of course us basement dwellers and graveyard shifters never dared daydream we'd draw that lottery luck to head off-world first, before the death wave radiation arrived. I'm bracing now for the inevitable unrest soon. Fracturing stability further when mass disappointment boils over at evacuation restrictions guaranteed too sparse for populations, unable to be placated by speeches about hope, future, and optimism.

I've been asked to overview ghost migration projections to inform off-world colonization procedures - even eons away my otherworldly talents may be indispensable. Here's hoping ghosts fare smooth in re-homing queues.

In the meantime, I'm better focused continuing my investigations and tying loose ends before disaster derails closure completely. Time now to settle affairs under Earth skies before the great exodus shuffle scatters all threads of memory and meaning irretrievably between the stars.

[03-24-2034] Little Green Neighbors

With global unrest rising awaiting revelation of Earth evacuation contingencies, the government finally disclosed our interstellar neighbors' physical nature through footage of various spacecraft hangars and envoy delegations.

Got to admit, it was hard not bursting into nervous laughter at the cliche little green men through the glimpse - bulbous insectoid eyes wrapping cranial smooth carapaces glistening like jade, trios of spindly fingers gesturing in herky-jerky pantomime. Even their quilted uniforms looked snatched from a bad sci-fi matinee serial. Their craft reminded me of flying hubcaps in bad post-Atomic movies. Hopefully just as much translating error as good faith kitsch.

But behind each uncanny smile, contrasts clicked - vastly alien psyches peered through such familiar stereotype skins at frightened cattle awaiting numeric judgment. Those inscrutable owl eyes held neither malice nor sympathy as they clinically scanned the reaction.

Some Pentagon emissary asked my psychic read of their visitors with society cracking under salvation mystery pressure. But even without direct contact, the vibe beamed clearly - they remained scientifically dispassionate delivering extinction notices and survival lottery chances, not companionship. Maybe refugee shelters will prove more hospitable than that.

[03-25-2034] Bugging Out To The Stars.

Today's shocking broadcast bulletin finally disclosed logistics for an Earth evacuation contingency using the aliens' interstellar transport network to settle willing refugee groups on one of their colony worlds. Vague descriptors like "habitability certification" and "biosphere compatibility apprenticeships" underscored this arrangement's stringent assimilation requirements, but beggars can't be choosers with our sun hot on death's door.

Few concrete details were given on precisely how many people could integrate aboard their vessels, but the promise of continued existence outweighed the anonymity of destinations sight-unseen for most. Personally I'd saddle up on the first zig-zagging saucer out of here to escape the news camera crews stirring mass panic and preying on wavering public psyches like vultures.

This planet's bound to be a right ghost town soon between celestial exile ships jumping Earth's best and brightest to the unknown and civil unrest claiming who remains. But a few straggler specters hitching starbound rides surely beats the prospect of keeping ectoplasmic peace amongst Snake Plissken level abandoned habitats down here across the death wave radiation fallout. Better pray we don't bottleneck too hard at off-world arrival immigration gates.

No shortage now of self-nominated "visionaries" and their pedestalled talking heads convening futile subcommittees on 24/7 news channels debating colony selection protocols and resource quotas - as if grandstanding could secure their family a starboard seat when this sun sinks.

But despite bureaucratic illusions of control, exodus urgency will sort evacuees more on practical skill sets than political sway or bank accounts when launch day manifests get announced. Teachers and surgeons before senators. Allegedly. So I'll stick to current spectral wrangling duties rather than waste energy lobbying selection boards. Time and death catch all equal - best prepare prompt reports for my resettlement resume highlighting 'spectral integration case studies'. Surely off-world infrastructure needs ethereal environment impact guidance? Let's hope spirits and aliens mingle peacefully.

In the meantime though, ever-growing mass unrest floods both human streets and limbo's alleyways pending revelation of the chosen few. And you can scarcely requisition decent coffee standing between those twin desperation pressures. With any luck, our narrow-skulled administrators will finally publicize substantive evacuation details before society snaps beyond all salvation.

Government sites crashed under the query spikes when so-called "priority evacuation criteria" were published today. Supposedly technical experts and creative talents deemed "vital to species continuity" get heavy preference to the coveted off-world colony lifeboats. Though practical spectral management skills seem conspicuously absent.

Politicians undoubtedly already claimed premium stasis bunks for their lineages prescribing such exclusionary standards. This "lottery" intends to placate desperate masses by pretending to offer fair fortune's favor. But the system mathematically stacks against nearly all from the start. They forget a few of us provide legitimate interdimensional infrastructure guidance when colonizing unknown realms.

Of course my services remain grounded here with the rest sentenced to ride out the apocalypse timeline. But I will continue assisting local specters through the End Times rather than beg statistical odds algorithmically excluding most. If Earth's final ghosts aren't barred from accompanying their tethered soul groups to the stars, perhaps modest medium credentials still hold sway arguing evacuation petitions. Though by now, I expect the last ships will have fled by that stage.

Surely outraged souls gravitationally reflect back here, their fury at shattered terrestrial tethers anchoring them to echo within these abandoned ruins even as living refugee ships flee across stellar seas. None can escape the system-wide uprooting, neither body nor spirit.

Headlines heralded the Secretary General's urgent revelations promising "long awaited" evacuation specifics. But as the vaguely labeled livestream video buffered, the tide already turned – even our puffed-up public leaders felt outmatched moving Earth's expiry hourglass now.

When the Secretary General solemnly revealed evacuation specifics, his words barely penetrated the anticipatory din…

…transport capacity would support only 5,000 initial refugees as an absolute maximum limit.

No embellishment could eclipse the bleakness of that announcement. I connected dots of family, orphans, homeless, now nothing more than death row statistics. Billions sentenced from worlds away by cold math and scarcely more accommodation than spectral steerage. What were their grand plans to quell riots when people realized golden lottery propaganda only placated temporarily? But tongues held hostage make for poor peacekeepers.

In one address, I watched hope gutted beyond reconciliation outside corruption catchments. All paths now shotgun down despair, measured only by twisted means of getting there. This was no "darkest before dawn". Just a long dusk burning unjustly against the meek. I'd spend my remaining wisps of light comforting spirits set to wander even interstellar black in search of sanctuary rarely found. A drop in this flood, all soothers stretch inadequate, but solemn purpose persisting nonetheless as society's needed anchor point holding fast.

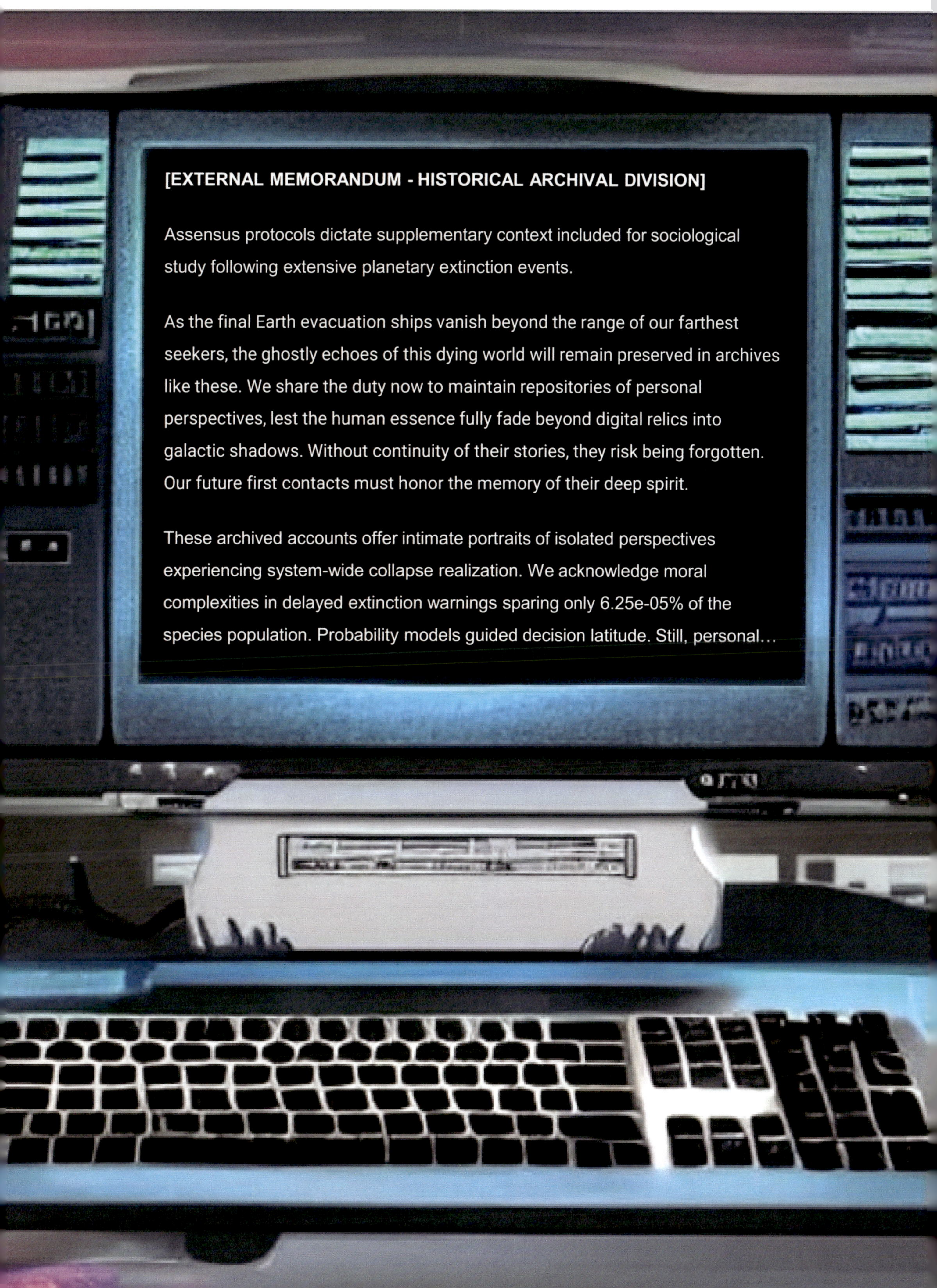

[EXTERNAL MEMORANDUM - HISTORICAL ARCHIVAL DIVISION]

Assensus protocols dictate supplementary context included for sociological study following extensive planetary extinction events.

As the final Earth evacuation ships vanish beyond the range of our farthest seekers, the ghostly echoes of this dying world will remain preserved in archives like these. We share the duty now to maintain repositories of personal perspectives, lest the human essence fully fade beyond digital relics into galactic shadows. Without continuity of their stories, they risk being forgotten. Our future first contacts must honor the memory of their deep spirit.

These archived accounts offer intimate portraits of isolated perspectives experiencing system-wide collapse realization. We acknowledge moral complexities in delayed extinction warnings sparing only 6.25e-05% of the species population. Probability models guided decision latitude. Still, personal…

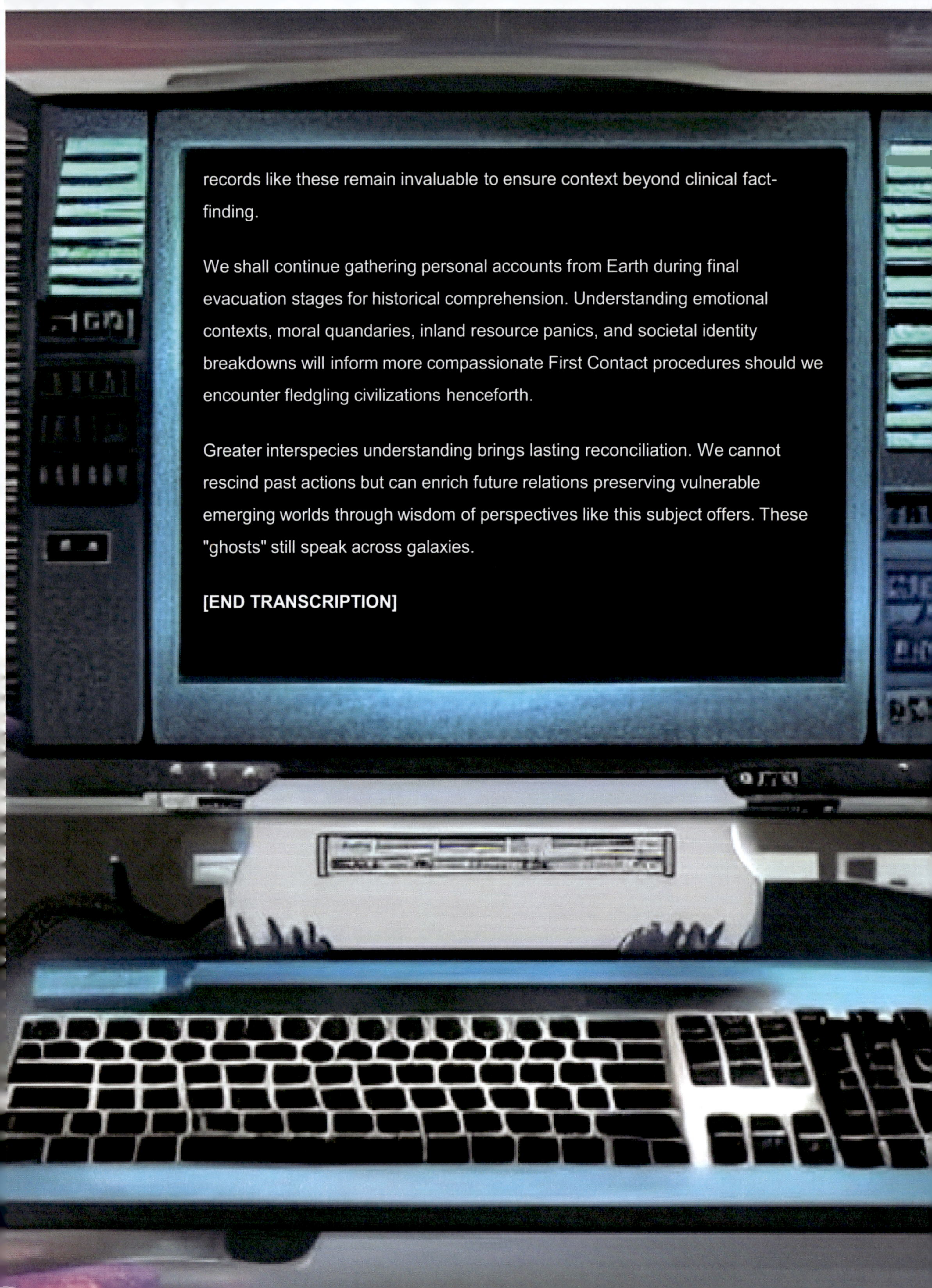

records like these remain invaluable to ensure context beyond clinical fact-finding.

We shall continue gathering personal accounts from Earth during final evacuation stages for historical comprehension. Understanding emotional contexts, moral quandaries, inland resource panics, and societal identity breakdowns will inform more compassionate First Contact procedures should we encounter fledgling civilizations henceforth.

Greater interspecies understanding brings lasting reconciliation. We cannot rescind past actions but can enrich future relations preserving vulnerable emerging worlds through wisdom of perspectives like this subject offers. These "ghosts" still speak across galaxies.

[END TRANSCRIPTION]

UNDER THE ELULGLIB EYE

DIR: LUCIENNE LEBEAU

DAWN.

THE LIGHT FROM ELULGLIB'S TWIN SUNS ASSAULTED LISA'S EYES. SHE GRUNTED AND TURNED OVER IN BED, AWAY FROM THE VENETIAN BLINDS. HOW DARE THEY LET ANY SUNLIGHT THROUGH. PUTTING HER HAND OVER HER EYES WOULDN'T BE ENOUGH. SHE GRABBED HER SLEEP MASK INSTEAD, GIVING HER ROOM A NASTY LOOK AS IF THE RETRO-STYLE BLINDS AND DIGITAL ART ON THE WALLS HAD WOKEN HER UP ON PURPOSE. SHE GLOWERED AT THE SCREENS DEPICTING EARTH'S SOOTHING LANDSCAPES AND FOR A MOMENT, HER HEART MOURNED.

SHE PUT ON HER MASK AND PLUNKED BACK DOWN ONTO HER PILLOWS, FALLING INTO A PEACEFUL LITTLE DROWSE, THINKING HOW LOVELY IT WOULD BE TO TAKE A LONG REST.

EXCEPT GARY CAME INTO THE BEDROOM, WIDE AWAKE AND HUMMING A TUNE, AND OPENED THE BLINDS. "WAKE UP, MY LOVE," HE SAID. "BREAKFAST IS SERVED."

THE SMELL OF COFFEE BROUGHT LISA TO SIT UP AS SHE HEARD A CLATTER OF A TRAY ON THE STANDING TABLE AND THE WOOSH OF THE BLINDS OPENING. GARY HAD PREPARED HER A VEGETARIAN DELIGHT—SOYA SAUSAGES, FARM FRESH EGGS FROM A BIRD QUITE SIMILAR TO A CHICKEN, TOAST, AND A GRANOLA-YOGURT PARFAIT WITH BERRIES. HE EVEN THREW IN HALF A GRAPEFRUIT-LIKE CITRUS, WITH A SMATTERING OF SUGAR ON TOP.

AS THE PICTURES ON THE WALL SCROLLED FROM THE BRAZILIAN RAINFOREST TO THE GRAND CANYON, MOUNT EVEREST, AND TRANQUIL LAKES AND STREAMS LISA HAD ONCE TRAVELED (THEY WERE FROM HER COLLECTION, AFTER ALL), SHE TURNED HER ATTENTION BACK TO GARY AND THE TRAY OF FOOD. HE'D BEEN SO THOUGHTFUL, EVEN SETTING HER TABLET IN FRONT OF HER AS THEY SAT TOGETHER AND ENJOYED THE QUIET ATMOSPHERE.

QUIET EXCEPT FOR THE DISTINCT HUMMING. THE PLANET SEEMED TO HAVE AN UNDERCURRENT OF HUMS THAT HUMANS COULD HEAR, BUT THE ALIENS HAD EITHER TUNED IT OUT OR IT WAS BELOW THEIR REGISTER. LISA WORKED TO IGNORE IT BUT THERE WERE MOMENTS IT FILLED HER CHEST, GIVING HER A CLAWING ANXIETY, A HEAVINESS THAT WORE INTO HER SOUL.

STARTING HER GRAPEFRUIT, LISA REACHED FOR THE SLEEK, TRANSLUCENT TABLET, ITS SURFACE COMING ALIVE WITH A RAINBOW OF COLORS. "GOOD MORNING, LISA LANGE-BENSON," IT SAID. "WOULD YOU LIKE TO READ THE NEWS?"

"PLEASE," SHE SAID. WITHOUT ANOTHER WORD, THE APP OPENED AND THE FIRST HEADLINE GREETED HER.....

EARTH FALLS TO SUPERNOVA SUN

LISA GAVE OUT A LITTLE GASP. THE NEWS CLAIMED EARTH, THEIR HOME, HAD BEEN CONFIRMED DESTROYED BY THE SUPERNOVA, AS PREDICTED BY THE ELULGLIBIANS. A SINGLE TEAR SLIPPED DOWN HER CHEEK. HOME WAS GONE.

A SIP OF COFFEE—ONE OF SEVERAL THINGS THE ELULGLIBIANS HAD MANAGED TO SAVE ON THEIR JOURNEY FROM EARTH—MADE THINGS FEEL SOMEWHAT BETTER.

"THEY TOLD US THEY PICKED THE BRIGHTEST AMONG US," LISA SAID.

"THEY TOLD US A LOT OF THINGS," GARY PUT HIS HAND ON HER BACK AND RUBBED IT, THEN GAVE HER SHOULDER A SQUEEZE. "ARE YOU OKAY?"

SHE SIGHED. "I GUESS SO. I WILL BE. I JUST—THE PLANET HAD 8 BILLION PEOPLE ON IT AND ONLY FIVE THOUSAND PEOPLE GOT TO LEAVE. IT JUST—I DIDN'T REALIZE JUST HOW AWFUL IT WOULD BE."

"A WISE MAN ONCE SAID:'DON'T THROW AWAY YOUR SUFFERING. TOUCH YOUR SUFFERING. FACE IT DIRECTLY, AND YOUR JOY WILL BECOME DEEPER. YOU KNOW THAT SUFFERING AND JOY ARE BOTH IMPERMANENT.' THICH NHAT HANH. OR BUDDHA. I MEAN, ONE OF THEM." GARY PUT HIS HANDS TOGETHER IN A'NAMASTE' POSE.

LISA ROLLED HER EYES. "THAT WISE MAN IS DEAD LIKE THE REST OF THEM. THEY DIDN'T EVEN BOTHER TAKING ANY SPIRITUAL LEADERS. THEY TOOK RICH ASSHOLES LIKE US AND CONFLATED IT WITH INTELLIGENCE. THIS PLACE SUCKS, GARE. I HATE IT."

GARY FROWNED. "I'M SORRY HONEY. BUT YOU AND I ARE INTELLIGENT."

"I AM," SHE SAID. HIS FROWN DEEPENED.

"WE BOTH ARE."

"YEAH." SHE WENT BACK TO HER BREAKFAST, PICKING AT THE SOYA SAUSAGES AND LOSING HERSELF IN THOUGHT. WHEN SHE LOOKED UP AGAIN AT THE DIGITAL PAINTINGS ON THE WALL, SHE SAW A FLASH OF SOMETHING. AN ALIEN FACE, HOLDING A SCALPEL, BLOOD FLYING AND SPATTERING ONTO THE SCREEN.

DOOM.

"LISA—LISA!" GARY SAID. HE WAS IN HER FACE, HOLDING HER ARMS AND SHAKING HER. SHE STARTLED, LOOKING AROUND THE KITCHEN. HOW DID SHE WIND UP IN THE KITCHEN?

"LISA-LISA!" GARY SAID. HE WAS IN HER FACE, HOLDING HER ARMS AND SHAKING HER. SHE STARTLED, LOOKING AROUND THE KITCHEN. HOW DID SHE WIND UP IN THE KITCHEN?

"I-GARY-WHAT HAPPENED?" LISA ASKED. HER HEAD FELT FOGGY, LIKE SHE NEEDED TO GO BACK TO SLEEP.

"I THINK YOU HAD A SEIZURE AGAIN," HE SAID. "WE NEED TO TAKE YOU TO THE HEALTH CENTER."

"LATER," LISA SHOOK HER HEAD. "JUST GIVE ME MY PILL. I FORGOT TO TAKE IT LAST NIGHT."

GARY GAVE HER A DISAPPROVING LOOK AND HANDED HER THE BOTTLE OF TABLETS. SHE DRY SWALLOWED ONE AND LOOKED AROUND THE ROOM. "WHAT TIME IS IT?"

"IT'S STILL MORNING. YOU JUST WANDERED OUT HERE WITH A BLANK LOOK ON YOUR FACE. I KNEW IT WAS A SEIZURE." GARY POINTED TO HIS WATCH. "FOUR MINUTES AND THIRTY-SIX SECONDS THIS TIME. WELL, FROM THE TIME YOU WANDERED IN HERE."

LISA LOOKED AROUND THE CHROME AND NEON KITCHEN, TRYING TO ORIENT HERSELF. GARY PLAYED WITH HIS ANTIQUE PERCOLATOR, MAKING ANOTHER POT OF COFFEE. IT STOOD OUT AS AN ODD RELIC AMIDST THE ADVANCED TECHNOLOGY. THOUGH HE WAS TRYING TO HIDE IT FROM HER, HIS FACE WAS NEVER INSCRUTABLE TO HER. HE WAS CONCERNED, WHETHER HE WOULD ADMIT IT OR NOT.

SHE WAS CLUTCHING HER TABLET STILL, THE SEIZURE HAD CAUSED HER MUSCLES TO CONTRACT TIGHTLY AROUND IT AS IF IT WERE A LIFE PRESERVER. "GARY, LOOK AT THIS, THOUGH. THIS ISN'T RIGHT. I CALCULATED THIS RIGHT BEFORE MY SEIZURE. EVEN WITH THE ELULGIBIAN TECH THEY COULDN'T MAKE AN ACTUAL CONFIRMATION, BUT THEY INSIST THE SUN IS GONE."

GARY TOOK THE TABLET FROM HER AND READ OVER THE ARTICLE. "WELL, MAYBE THEY CAN CONFIRM IT—WE DON'T REALLY KNOW HOW EXTENSIVE THE TECH THEY HAVE IS."

LISA SIGHED AND SHOOK HER HEAD. "I DON'T KNOW—IT JUST SEEMS TOO NICE AND NEAT TO ME."

"I DON'T DOUBT YOUR INSTINCTS," GARY SAID. "OR YOUR MATHEMATICS. WE SHOULD DIG DEEPER."

TOGETHER, THEY SCOURED THE ELULGLIBNET, A VAST DIGITAL OCEAN OF INFORMATION FROM BOTH THEIR WORLD AND THE ALIENS' WORLD. THEIR SEARCH UNEARTHED A HIDDEN GEM.

MIDNIGHT REPOSITORY

"MIDNIGHT REPOSITORY," SHE READ ALOUD. IT WAS A BLOG PENNED BY SOMEONE NAMED ALBY, A NAME THAT ECHOED IN LISA'S MIND, INTIMATE AND FAMILIAR. THE BLOG WAS A DIGITAL EPITAPH FOR EARTH, DETAILING ITS...

...LAST DAYS, THE CHOSEN FEW, AND THE HEART-WRENCHING ABANDONMENT OF BILLIONS.

LISA'S EYES, SCANNING THE BLOCKS OF TEXT, FROZE ON A HAUNTING PHRASE EMBEDDED IN AN OLDER ENTRY: "WAKE UP, LISA. WAKE UP." IT WAS LIKE A WHISPER FROM BEYOND, A SECRET MESSAGE MEANT ONLY FOR HER.

"DO YOU SEE IT, GARY?" SHE ASKED, POINTING TO HER SCREEN.

"SEE WHAT?" GARY SAID, HEARING THE PANIC CLIMB IN HER VOICE. "WHAT, HONEY? IT'S JUST A BLOG. BESIDES, I CAN'T SEE ANYTHING AT ALL. NOT LIKE THIS."

LISA LOOKED UP AT HIM, AND FOR A MOMENT, THE BRIEFEST FLASH, GARY'S FACE HAD NO EYES. THEY WERE SEWN SHUT.

THE TABLET SEEMED TO LEAP OUT OF HER HANDS AS SHE JUMPED, AND GARY LOOKED NORMAL AGAIN. STARTLED, BUT NORMAL. HIS EYES WERE STILL THERE.

"WAKE UP, LISA," SHE SAID, TAKING A STEP BACK. "I HAVE TO WAKE UP."

"NO," GARY TOOK A STEP TOWARDS HER. "LISA, IT'S JUST AN AFTEREFFECT OF THE SEIZURE. THIS IS REAL. YOU'RE REAL. REMEMBER? IT'S SURVIVOR'S GUILT COUPLED WITH EPILEPSY. HERE, JUST TAKE A SIP OF WATER AND A FEW DEEP BREATHS."

LISA LOOKED AROUND THE ROOM, TRYING TO REMEMBER. GARY'S HANDS GRASPED HER ARMS. THEY WERE WARM. SOOTHING. SOFT. HE FELT REAL. HE SMELLED OF THE COLOGNE SHE GOT HIM FOR HIS BIRTHDAY, JUST BEFORE THEY ENTERED THE SHIP THAT WOULD TAKE THEM FROM EARTH TO ELULGLIB.

HER MIND GRASPED THAT MEMORY AS TIGHTLY AS GARY'S GRIP ON HER ARMS. THE TALL AND ELEGANT ELULGLIBIANS, WITH THEIR BULBOUS HEADS AND WIDE BLACK EYES, HAD GENTLE HANDS, LOVINGLY STRAPPING THEM INTO THE SHIP. ONE OF THEM EVEN KISSED HER ON THE FOREHEAD TO REASSURE HER. "YOU WILL SLEEP," THEY SAID. "AND WHEN YOU AWAKE, YOU WILL BE SAFE ON OUR PLANET. ARE YOU REASSURED?"

LISA HAD NODDED, THOUGH INSIDE, HER NERVES JUMPED AND STRAINED AGAINST THE RESTRAINTS. THEN, A WARM AND SOOTHING FEELING WASHED OVER HER AS THE INJECTION OF THE SEDATIVE TOOK OVER. SHE HAD CLOSED HER EYES, AND WHEN SHE WOKE UP, SHE WAS IN A PROCESSING CENTER, RECEIVING A BEAUTIFUL HOME, PAIRED WITH GARY, AND WORKING ON SHARING THEIR TECHNOLOGY ON ROBOTICS. WELL, HER TECHNOLOGY ON ROBOTICS, ANYWAY.

SHE SETTLED DOWN AND GARY LOOSENED HIS GRIP. "BETTER?"

LISA NODDED. "BETTER."

PICKING UP THE TABLET, SHE WANDERED BACK INTO THE BEDROOM. "I THINK I SHOULD LIE DOWN FOR A BIT."

"THAT WOULD BE BEST. I'LL BE IN THE ART ROOM. I HAD AN IDEA FOR AN ILLUSTRATED STORY I WANTED TO TRY. IT'S ABOUT A TECH GURU WHO MEETS HIS MATCH IN A CYBERNETICIST AND THEY FALL MADLY IN LOVE." HE GRINNED AT HER. "YOU KNOW, LIKE US."

LISA CHUCKLED. "LET ME GUESS—YOU NAMED THEM JERRY AND LYSSA, RIGHT?"

GARY BLUSHED. "NO," HE SAID, MOCK DEFENSIVELY. "I NAMED THEM GERALD AND LEENA."

THAT MADE LISA LAUGH HARDER. "OKAY BUDDY. YOU GO DO THAT. I'LL BE OKAY."

SHE LIED SMOOTHLY TO HIM. EVERYTHING INSIDE OF HER WAS SCREAMING THAT IT WAS FAR FROM OKAY. SOMETHING WASN'T RIGHT AND SHE KNEW IT. CRAWLING INTO BED, SHE WAITED FOR GARY TO LEAVE AND WENT BACK TO HER TABLET. SHE POURED OVER MIDNIGHT REPOSITORY, READING EVERY ENTRY, TRYING TO REMEMBER WHAT LIFE WAS LIKE ON EARTH, WHY THEY COULD ONLY TAKE FIVE THOUSAND OF THEM, AND WHAT HER LIFE HAD BEEN LIKE WHEN SHE ARRIVED.

IT FELT LIKE SHE WAS LOOKING AT PIECES OF MEMORIES IN SHARDS, A KALEIDOSCOPE OF FRACTURED PICTURES AND HALF-HEARD VOICES. THE SUDDEN DEATH OF THEIR FRIEND, CHRIS, WHO DIDN'T SURVIVE THE TRANSIT, BRINGING THEIR NUMBER TO 4,999. BEING ABLE TO ACTUALLY COUNT THE DWINDLING NUMBER OF HUMANS SOBERED HER. SHE REMEMBERED THEM ENCOURAGING HER AND GARY TO BREED. THEY'D BEEN TRYING, BUT GETTING NOWHERE. SHE WONDERED HOW LONG IT WOULD TAKE, AND IF THEY WOULD GROW IMPATIENT WITH THEM NOT BREEDING. THEY SEEMED TO BE KEEN ON REPOPULATING, PROMISING THAT THEY WOULD TERRAFORM A NEW PLACE. A SAFE PLACE JUST LIKE EARTH, BUT BEFORE THE FALL. THEY WOULD CALL IT "EDEN."

HOW LONG HAD IT BEEN SINCE THAT PROMISE WAS MADE, AND HOW MANY OF THEM WERE ACTUALLY LEFT?

THERE WAS A MEETING FOR THE REMAINING HUMANS BUT A WEEK BEFORE, AND SOMETHING ABOUT IT FELT OFF. EVEN THEN. LISA WAS LATE, PERHAPS PREGNANT. SHE THOUGHT ABOUT IT. DIDN'T THEY ACTUALLY HAVE TWO CHILDREN?

HER HEAD SWAM AND SHE LOST CONSCIOUSNESS.

"WAKE UP, LISA. LISA? WAKE UP," GARY'S VOICE, BUT IT WAS FAR AWAY. WHY WAS HE FAR AWAY?

OPENING HER EYES, MIDNIGHT REPOSITORY WAS DISPLAYED ON EVERY SCREEN IN THE BEDROOM. ALBY'S SARCASTIC FACE AND THE WORDS WAKE UP LISA EMBLAZONED ON EVERY ONE. ON HER TABLET, ON THE SCREENS, AND EVEN IN THE WINDOWS WHEN SHE RIPPED BACK THE BLINDS.

PANIC AND REALIZATION COLLIDED WITHIN HER. "THIS ISN'T REAL," SHE GASPED, THE ROOM SPINNING AROUND HER. "THIS ISN'T REAL, GARE!"

SHE RAN TO THE KITCHEN. GARY WAS STANDING THERE, IN FRONT OF THE TRAY THAT WAS STILL SITTING ON THE KITCHEN ISLAND. "WAKE UP, LISA. WAKE UP, LISA. WAKE UP, LISA," HE SAID. HE WASN'T LOOKING AT HER. HIS VOICE HAD BEEN REPLACED WITH A ROBOTIC, TINNY NOISE, ON REPEAT, AN ENTREATMENT FOR HER TO WAKE UP.

IN A MOMENT OF TERRIFYING CLARITY, SHE GRABBED THE GRAPEFRUIT SPOON ON THE TRAY, ITS EDGES GLINTING IN THE NEON PINK AND BLUE OF THE KITCHEN.

"REMEMBER THAT MOVIE? THERE IS NO SPOON," SHE SAID, TRYING TO WILL IT INTO BENDING. "THERE IS NO SPOON. THERE IS NO SPOON."

IT DIDN'T YIELD AND GARY LOOKED AT HER WITH BEWILDERMENT IN HIS EYES, SNAPPING OUT OF THE ROBOTIC LOOP. "LISA, WHAT THE HELL?"

SHE CLUTCHED THE SPOON IN A DEATH GRIP AND RAN AROUND THE KITCHEN ISLAND. GARY FOLLOWED HER. "HONEY, PLEASE. YOU NEED TO CALM DOWN. TAKE YOUR PILL. YOU'RE GOING TO HAVE ANOTHER SEIZURE."

LISA STOPPED IN HER TRACKS AND LAUGHED, RISING TO HYSTERICS.   WITH A CRY THAT MINGLED FEAR AND DETERMINATION, SHE PLUNGED THE SPOON INTO GARY'S CHEST AND THEN HER OWN THROAT.

K A B L A M !

THE WORLD AROUND HER SHATTERED INTO SHARP PIECES AND LISA AWOKE STRAPPED TO A COLD, METALLIC TABLE, HER BODY ACHING. THE ELULGLIBIANS TOWERED OVER HER, THEIR ELONGATED FORMS GROTESQUE AND TERRIFYING, EMITTING A SYMPHONY OF UNNERVING SOUNDS. THEIR LANGUAGE, CLICKS AND LONG VOWEL SOUNDS THAT RATTLED THE TABLE UNDER HER BACK.

THAT FAMILIAR HUM OF THE PLANET RATTLED IN HER EARS—IT WAS—WHAT WAS IT?

REFRIGERATORS AND BLAST CHILLERS ALL AROUND THE EXPANSIVE KITCHEN. LISA PANICKED, WISHING IN EARNEST THAT SHE HADN'T WOKEN UP.

SHE TRIED TO SIT UP, TO LOOK AROUND, BUT COULD ONLY RAISE HER NECK AS HER TORSO WAS FIRMLY CHAINED TO THE TABLE. "GARY? WHERE ARE YOU?"

TO HER HORROR, GARY WAS DISPLAYED AS A MACABRE CENTERPIECE ON A STEEL KITCHEN ISLAND, AN APPLE-LIKE FRUIT STUFFED IN HIS MOUTH, HIS EYES VOID OF LIFE. THE ALIENS APPROACHED, THEIR CLICKING INTENSIFYING, AS ONE OF THEM RAISED A BLUNT OBJECT OVER HER.

LISA'S SCREAM TORE THROUGH THE AIR, A LONE HUMAN CRY AGAINST THE ALIEN CACOPHONY. THE HAMMER TO HER HEAD WAS SWIFT, THE PAIN SHARP AS THE LIGHTS WENT OUT. DARKNESS CLAIMED HER, SWALLOWING HER ECHO INTO THE DEPTHS OF ELULGLIB.

"THIS PAIR COULD NOT BREED," DORLAK SAID TO HIS YOUNG APPRENTICE. "SHE WAS NOT FERTILE ENOUGH AND HIS SPERM COUNT WAS TOO LOW. THIS IS WHY WE TOOK SO MANY BREEDING PAIRS. ALAS, IT WAS NOT MEANT TO BE. HOWEVER, DUE TO THEIR OPULENT LIFESTYLES AND HEALTH CONSCIOUSNESS, THIS PAIR WILL MAKE FOR A DELICIOUS REPAST FOR OUR QUEEN, AND WE CAN CLONE THE ORGANS.."

THE APPRENTICE NODDED. "THE HUMANS WERE SO EASILY FOOLED," SHE SAID. "BUT TELL ME, SIR DORLAK, DID THEIR SUN REALLY GO SUPERNOVA?"

DORLAK CLICKED HIS AMUSEMENT. "I REALLY DON'T KNOW, EMAXIE. YOU'D HAVE TO ASK THE HUNTERS ABOUT THEIR JOURNEY AND HOW THEY ENSNARED THE HUMANS. I SIMPLY KNOW THEY WERE WIDE-EYED FOOLS WHO THOUGHT THEY WERE GENIUSES. A ROBOTICS EXPERT, THIS ONE. SHE WAS ADVANCED FOR EARTH, BUT LEAGUES BEHIND ELULGLIB IN TECHNOLOGY. GULLIBLE, THE LOT OF THEM."

HE GAVE IT A THOUGHT AS HE RIPPED OPEN THE TORSO AND PULLED OUT HER INTESTINES. "I DON'T THINK SO, YET," HE SAID. "I MEAN, THEY DO COME IN SHIPMENTS OF FIVE-THOUSAND AT A TIME. IT'S ALL WE CAN CARRY WITHOUT REACHING MAXIMUM PAYLOAD TO GET OUT OF EARTH'S ORBIT. AT LEAST THAT'S WHAT ONE OF THE INTERSTELLAR EXPERTS TOLD ME WHILE I FED HIM A LOVELY ADOLESCENT LIVER PÂTÉ."

EMAXIE CHITTERED. "I COULD ALMOST FEEL SORRY FOR THEM," SHE SAID, TASTING A SAMPLE OF THE KIDNEY SHE HAD JUST HARVESTED. "BUT THEY'RE TOO DELICIOUS."

and
OUR FEATURE
PRESENTATION

DOUBLE FEATURE presents:
Son of the monolith
dir: JOHN A. McCOLLEY

"Son of the Monolith"
was the planned, but unproduced sequel to the 1957 film
"The Monolith Monsters"

DOUBLE FEATURE's crack team of researchers and archivists were able to unearth portions of its script, AND from those remnants...
author John A. McColley has been able to reproduce the narrative for you, for the first time...

"Hey, Dr. Miller! I brought my cousin, Arvin. Arvin, this is Doc. Miller, hero of San Angelo."

"Now let's not get carried away, Jim," the tall, middle-aged man said, squinting from the shade of a majestic white building with columns to either side of the stairs into the desert sun to see them as they approached from either side of a dinged-up old pickup truck. "I did what I could, saved some people, failed to save others. Nothing anyone else wouldn't do in my situation."

"You're too modest, doc. I bet that girl's parents would agree."

"Maybe, maybe, but now we've got a horrendous mess to pick up. The Army's taken away all the crystal from the monoliths, but there's still destroyed buildings, cars, the dam... Speaking of which, that's where I'm headed. Thanks for coming by to clean up the office. So many lost samples, so much broken equipment. It's going to take me months to recover, years, but cleaning up is step one. Don't forget your masks and gloves. You don't want to breath even the tiniest specks of that crystal in. Just get everything into this dumpster over here and someone will be along to empty it. Everything's going into a secure dump site the Army's setting up."

"Don't you worry, doc. We'll have this place looking like new by the end of the day," Jim promised. He glanced at Arvin who nodded his agreement. They were getting paid, after all.

"I would appreciate it. That's a better timeline than we have for the dam, or the water towers. It's going to be bottled water and showers over in Fayette for a couple of weeks, I'm afraid."

"We'll get by, and San Angelo will be back on its feet in no time, just watch!" Jim said excitedly.

"If we can find more with your positive attitude, I'm sure that's true, Jim. Good luck with it. If you have any trouble, call up to the dam. The number's in the book of instructions and reminders I left on the front desk."

"Sure thing, doc!" Jim said with a wave as Dr. Miller got into his Jeep and started the engine. With one last wave, he was off, dodging chunks of concrete and piles of brick left in the wake of the strange event some were calling an "attack." Jim didn't know about that, but he was grateful for the work and that his parents house had been out of the path of destruction.

"A book? Is he serious?" Arvin asked, staring down at the half-inch thick stack of papers set into a three-ring binder. Jim shrugged. He admired both Dr. Miller and Arvin for different reasons, in different ways. Arvin was the older cousin he'd looked up to since he was little. The boy had sneaked him his first beer, first cigarette, had convinced him to ask Becky Taylor out... But Dr. Miller seemed to know everything about everything else: chemistry, rocks, how to overcome mysterious illnesses, and how to fix dams.

"I mean... the man knows his science. I know some of the samples he had from before the attack were toxic, arsenic and mercury and the like. And he's not wrong about the monoliths. A few people were straight turned to stone, or something like it. They woulda died for sure if he didn't help them. They might look dorky, but I think we should wear the masks and stuff." "Whatever..." Arvin said with a note of disdain that made Jim cringe, but then the older boy slid the gas mask-like device over his head. Jim followed suit and they stared at one another for a moment.

"Ssshh! Ahhhh! Ssshhh!" Jim said, "Take me to your leader."

"Weeoooo Weeoooo!" Arvin said, his leather-gloved hands floating around like movie spacecraft. They both broke down laughing. After a minute, Arvin was calm enough to ask, "Do you think they were sent?"

"What? The Monoliths? Like some kind of actual attack or something?" Jim asked. Arvin shrugged.

"I dunno, maybe... Or maybe the government like released a gas or something. I've been reading, and it wouldn't be the first time."

"That you were reading?" Jim ribbed.

"No, seriously. They gassed whole towns before, with like chemicals that made people hallucinate."

"Look around, this wasn't a hallucination. The damage in here, sure, maybe someone goes a little crazy and trashes the place, but chunks of buildings knocked off? Peoples' houses flattened?" It bothered Jim that Arvin didn't believe him. He'd seen it with his own eyes, that should relative silence for a while, checking items off be good enough. They worked in the list of directives Dr. Miller had left, namely moving the

…twisted furniture out to the dumpster first, then smaller things like trash cans, then sweeping up and scrubbing out the smaller bits and dust from every crevice. There was even a spray bottle of stuff meant to neutralize the monolith shards if they came across any.

"Man, are you sure these cupboards aren't older than the rocks?" Arvin asked. Jim looked around at the geologist's office and had to agree. Everything was covered in dust like they were excavating an Egyptian tomb.

All the equipment and furniture and a lot of the samples had been smashed in the fuss of the last few weeks. Weird rocks had risen up like skyscrapers around San Angelo and fallen over, crushing everything in their paths.

People lit out like it was a wildfire, grabbing their kids and driving while they could. Now it was all over, everyone was settling in again, cleaning up. Arvin had been off visiting friends in Fayette. None of it had meant much to him until his cousin Jim had asked if he wanted to earn a good day's wage helping clean up. Jim was too much of a bookworm for Arvin, as much as he wanted to measure up to the older boy, but fifteen dollars a day was better than he would make at the gas station.

"Minerals, not rocks, and put your mask back on. There's all kinds of toxic stuff in here. All that dust you're kicking up could give ya cancer or somethin'," Jim warned.

"Dust? Now you sound like all those people who were afraid of space rocks. They're rocks, people. They just sit around."

"You weren't there. It was scary. They shot up to a hundred feet high and fell over, smashing trucks, Wilkins' gas station, houses left and right. The Army came and got the ones from in here. We're just cleaning up the normal stuff with masks and gloves, but they had big suits with helmets and everything, looked like they were goin' divin', '20,000 Leagues Under the Sea' style. If the army takes it that serious, you know it's bad news," Jim said.

"Whatever…" Arvin said with a note of disdain that made Jim cringe, but then the older boy slid the gas mask-like device over his head. Jim followed suit and they stared at one another for a moment.

"Ha ha, all right." Arvin pulled his mask down from atop his head. It made breathing harder, like the air was thick and damp. He'd never been to a swamp, but he imagined that's what it was like. They worked for hours, sweeping shards of glass from cupboard faces and beakers and minerals into buckets. They fought to untangle metal equipment that looked like floor lamps from some kind of hospital bed.

"What the heck happened here? What does a geologist need a hospital bed for?" Arvin asked.

"What?" Jim asked as he tilted his head to indicate they should roll it out the front door. Down a few stone steps to the sidewalk, they heaved it over the metal lip of the dumpster onto the pile of junk that had grown to impressive proportions. He hadn't realized the office was so big.

"This bed. Miller didn't sleep on it, did he? Tell me he's not a weirdo."

"Naw, I don't think so. The stones did somethin' to some people, like they were poison or somethin'. The doc tried to treat 'em. That's what I hear. How about we get that next pile of scales next to the counter and go get lunch?"

"Sounds good to me."

Back inside, they both grabbed buckets and threw the little brass weights in. Arvin spotted one squat cylinder at the base of the wall. "Don't suppose these are worth somethin', y' know, for scrap?" Arvin asked. Jim shrugged.

"Dunno, but I'm guessin' if the Army is takin' it all away to dump down a hole in the middle of nowhere, there's a chance it's dangerous." Arvin scoffed.

Reaching down, the glove kept Arvin's fingers from wrapping around the small, round, weight. He pulled the gauntlet off and tried again. Sharp pain lanced his finger and shot up his arm. He yanked his hand back. "Ah! Dammit!" He pushed up his mask. Droplets of blood splattered on the end of the counter and the floor. He stuck his finger in his mouth. He saw a flicker of movement like a wisp of smoke behind the brass weight and kicked at it, hitting only the base of the counter.

"What happened?" Jim asked.

"Damn rat bit me!" Arvin took his finger out and looked at it. Got me good. We got any bandages?"

"It was probably a piece of glass we missed. We can fix you up back at the house."

"Let's go then." Arvin, dropping his mask and gloves on the counter. He turned his hand back and forth, examining the cut, then pulled out his handkerchief and wrapped it. The wound pulsed.

"Just, uh, hold it up and keep pressure on it," Jim said.

***

Back at Jim's house, they went straight to the bathroom and unearthed the first aid kit from the closet. Arvin held his hand over the sink and unwound the handkerchief, sucking air between his teeth as the injury was disturbed. They rinsed the finger, but couldn't find a splinter or shard of glass to pull out. Jim put the tweezers down and picked up the brown peroxide bottle.

"You want a cotton ball or just a pour over?"

"Pouring's fine." Finger still over the sink, Jim tipped the bottle slowly, finally getting a little of the clear liquid to cascade over the scratch. It bubbled and hissed… and smoked a little? He was startled and pulled back. No, it had to be his imagination. They waited a few seconds, then rinsed off the chemical cleaner with water from the tap. Jim had never really considered the value in having a well, but his family would have water while everyone relying on the city's water would be out of luck for some time. Small blessings.

Jim pointed to a towel hanging on a bar at the side of the vanity. "Dry it off. If your finger's wet, the bandage won't stick."

"I know that," Arvin said testily, grabbing the terrycloth from his cousin. "Sorry, thanks for helping with this. It's not a very manly injury, but it still stings."

"Of course. I was a scout for a while, you know, first aid badge and everything. And plenty of chances to use it, what with whittling, fire starting, and cooking."

"Cooking, yeah, that reminds me. I'm starving," Arvin said.

"Ditto, let's grab something from the kitchen. I think Mom went shopping in Fayette last night. Everything in town is still closed. Or flattened."

They made heavily-piled sandwiches, wiping out the roast beef and ham from the fridge and sneaked a couple of beers each and a bag of chips. They drove out to the back of the ranch where the flat, dry, land dropped off into a canyon. One broad, reaching, oak tree stood near the brink, providing shade. Jim had never seen the crack in the earth filled with anything but tumbleweeds and dust devils, but now the floodwaters from the busted dam formed a salty lake.

"Man, I could use a dip," Arvin said, wiping his brow.

"Better not. Those weird minerals are still down there, and who knows what they're doin' to the water?" Jim said. "Besides, you ate so much you're gonna have to wait *two* hours before swimming instead of just one!" Shade and full bellies and beer brought

…drowsiness. Bees buzzed. The wind blew warm and slow. The teens dozed until the sun shone in their eyes.

"Aw crap, man, we musta fell asleep! Arvin, wake up!" Jim said, nudging his cousin.

"Nnnggg…"

"C'mon, man. If we're gonna get paid, we gotta get back and get at least a couple more hours' work in… Hey, what's wrong with you? You look sickly… almost… gray…" Jim gasped, scrambling across the truck bed to the back of the cab, clinking his beer bottles. The sound roused Arvin, whose face faded from healthy tan to desert stone over the course of seconds. The other boy pushed himself up, knocking his own beers over, spilling the dregs. The bubbling liquid washed over the hand which suddenly turned slate gray and began smoking. The hand grew in size. The arm followed quickly after.

Jim leapt for his life over the side of the truck bed, and took off across the scrubby prairie toward his house. Behind him, the truck's suspension creaked. A heavy footstep followed, then another. Tree branches rustled, then cracked alongside a grunt. One of the truck's tires exploded. Metal screamed. The tree creaked and cracked more.

A look over his shoulder turned into a stunned stare as he saw Arvin's head rise up through the canopy of the tree, then the tree leaned back and tumbled into the canyon.

"Arvin!" He cried out, reaching for his cousin, but the tree, the boy and the truck were all gone, Arvin's transformation causing the cliff to disintegrate. He tried to listen for them hitting the water, but he was too far away. Surely, the other teen couldn't have survived that fall, not with a truck and a tree falling on him, not even under the influence of the monolith. That had to be it, right? What else could it be?

He started walking, slowly, back to the site of the accident, to see if he could see anything, wondering what he would say to his aunt and uncle, to his parents… The truck, aww man, the truck… They were going to kill him.

Eventually, he stood looking down at the brown water. Could have been nothing down there, or a whole town submerged like in that movie he saw once. No one would ever know. But he would know. And the police would want to drag the slowly moving river, find the body, at any rate. Wasn't anyone's fault, he told himself, just another casualty of whatever weirdness had come over San Angelo lately.

Something broke the surface of the water, creating a small "v" shaped wave in the muddy water. Was it a hand? Had Arvin survived the fall after all? He would have to get a rope… no, there was nowhere to tie it off or wrap it around now the tree was gone, and there was no way he'd have been able to haul Arvin up on his own *before* he'd turned into a living statue. He had to get help, the phone, Doc Miller!

Jim turned to run back to the house when he heard a sound like fingernails on a chalkboard that grew louder by the second. After a few steps, he fell to his knees, hands clamped over his ears. The ground shook. Would more of the cliff collapse? He gritted his teeth and pushed himself to his feet, looking back as all the myths told him not to. A sword of gray stone pierced the sky, thrust from the waters below, and it wasn't the only one. A dozen others rose past the line of the cliff as he watched.

Jim took a step back, then another, before turning and running full out. He poured it on like he had in the track state championships two years before. It was more than two hundred yards to the house. His lunch pounded upward with every step, even as the piercing scream of the growing monoliths faded in the distance.

Within a stone's throw of the farmhouse, Jim was home free. He started to slow his pace, his pounding heart, burning lungs, and a stitch in his side reminding him that he had left off running too long. He was out of shape.

Boom! A wave of sound reverberated in his chest, rattling the windows, setting the wind chimes to jangling. A rain storm? Now?

Boom!

No, not rain, he didn't see any lighting to go with the thunder, and the strikes were too-

Boom! Brows knitting together, Jim turned to look back at the place where the old oak had stood for over a hundred years. Now, there was a gray tower, like some obscene modern abomination of architecture striding toward him

Arvin, if the thing was Arvin still, stood twice as tall as the tree where they'd parked. He looked head to foot like he was carved out of dark gray stone, a living statue which meant to crush Jim under his massive foot. There was no way the old wooden farmhouse was going to stop that thing. He'd never have time to get to the phone, get the operator to connect him to the dam offices, and explain what was happening to Doc Miller.

What else could he do? Jim thought quickly. His motorbike was in the garage. The muffler still had a hole in it, but the Sheriff pulling him over again was the least of his worries.

The ground shook again, hard. Crashes and clangs told Jim that pots and plates were falling off shelves in the kitchen, jostling out of cabinets. There was no time to worry about that, though. The next steps came quicker. Jim hauled the back door of the garage open. The cat shot out, a gold streak that tripped him up and sent him sprawling onto the concrete floor of the garage, scraping up his hands and left elbow. He pushed himself to his feet as oil cans and tools fell from their nails on the wall. He grabbed the keys off the hook and jumped on his bike, kicking it to life. Ginger was out of sight. He hoped she found a safe place to hide. Another thunderous stomp cut the thought short, bringing a shower of dust from the rafters and a clatter of hubcaps as a stack fell over.

Jim revved the engine and shot forward as wood creaked and gave way behind him. Splinters pelted off his back, jabbing into his neck as he wheeled around, setting himself in line with the driveway. He shot a look at the building. Over the low roof he saw an angular, twisted face which had once belonged to his cousin.

Hands like steam shovels came down on the garage, splitting it down …the middle and pushing it to either side. Jim gunned the engine and took off down the driveway trailing a plume of dust.

A few hundred yards later, where the old, rutted farm road met the state highway, Jim turned to look back again. Giant-Arvin had missed the farmhouse, but was picking up speed, ripping clods of dirt from the driveway with every step. Perhaps even more terrifying, Jim could see a forest of gray stone spreading across the field between the cliff and the house. Straight, sharp blades of gray were mixed with jagged and branching specimens. So much for their house being out of the way of the attack. He had to get to the Doc to let him know what was happening.

Nodding to himself, he turned right, away from town. He might find help in San Angelo, but he would also be leading the creature there to finish off the job the monoliths had started. Jim pushed through the fog of fear to try to focus on the geologist and the path to the new dam.

It would mean leading the creature to more water, too. He decided it was a chance he had to take, and set off. He rode hard to keep his distance from Arvin, but frequently glanced in the mirror. He looked forward again just in time to see the car pulling out in front of him. He swerved. The car clipped his rear wheel and the world spun, then slammed into him, hard. He felt bones crack in his lower leg and his chest. The world turned gray.

"What in God's green earth were you thinking, boy? You could have gotten yourself ki—oh, that leg doesn't look good at all," an older female voice said. "I'll go call an ambulance."

"No, no time," Jim tried to tell her. "Dr. Miller…"

"Mr. Miller isn't a doctor, hun, he just collects rocks and such."

"Minerals…," Miller had corrected him so many times since he'd been helping out at the temporary lab, that it was his last thought as pain overwhelmed him and the world faded to a gray fog.

"Wha? Where am I?" Jim woke, disoriented in a strange living room. His leg screamed with pain, while his ribs stabbed him with every breath.

Arvin, if the thing was Arvin still, stood twice as tall as the tree where they'd parked. He looked head to foot like he was carved out of dark gray stone, a living statue which meant to crush Jim under his massive foot. There was no way the old wooden farmhouse was going to stop that thing. He'd never have time to get to the phone, get the operator to connect him to the dam offices, and explain what was happening to Doc Miller.

What else could he do? Jim thought quickly. His motorbike was in the garage. The muffler still had a hole in it, but the Sheriff pulling him over again was the least of his worries.

The ground shook again, hard. Crashes and clangs told Jim that pots and plates were falling off shelves in the kitchen, jostling out of cabinets. There was no time to worry about that, though. The next steps came quicker. Jim hauled the back door of the garage open. The cat shot out, a gold streak that tripped him up and sent him sprawling onto the concrete floor of the garage, scraping up his hands and left elbow. He pushed himself to his feet as oil cans and tools fell from their nails on the wall. He grabbed the keys off the hook and jumped on his bike, kicking it to life. Ginger was out of sight. He hoped she found a safe place to hide. Another thunderous stomp cut the thought short, bringing a shower of dust from the rafters and a clatter of hubcaps as a stack fell over.

Jim revved the engine and shot forward as wood creaked and gave way behind him. Splinters pelted off his back, jabbing into his neck as he wheeled around, setting himself in line with the driveway. He shot a look at the building. Over the low roof he saw an angular, twisted face which had once belonged to his cousin.

Hands like steam shovels came down on the garage, splitting it down the middle and pushing it to either side. Jim gunned the engine and took off down the driveway trailing a plume of dust.

A few hundred yards later, where the old, rutted farm road met the state highway, Jim turned to look back again. Giant-Arvin had missed the farmhouse, but was picking up speed, ripping clods of dirt from the driveway with every step. Perhaps even more terrifying, Jim could see a forest of gray stone spreading across the field between the cliff and the house. Straight, sharp blades of gray were mixed with jagged and branching specimens. So much for their house being out of the way of the attack. He had to get to the Doc to let him know what was happening.

Nodding to himself, he turned right, away from town. He might find help in San Angelo, but he would also be leading the creature there to finish off the job the monoliths had started. Jim pushed through the fog of fear to try to focus on the geologist and the

paCCCCCCCCC

Hands like steam shovels came down on the garage, splitting it down the middle and pushing it to either side. Jim gunned the engine and took off down the driveway trailing a plume of dust.

A few hundred yards later, where the old, rutted farm road met the state highway, Jim turned to look back again. Giant-Arvin had missed the farmhouse, but was picking up speed, ripping clods of dirt from the driveway with every step. Perhaps even more terrifying, Jim could see a forest of gray stone spreading across the field between the cliff and the house. Straight, sharp blades of gray were mixed with jagged and branching specimens. So much for their house being out of the way of the attack. He had to get to the Doc to let him know what was happening.

Nodding to himself, he turned right, away from town. He might find help in San Angelo, but he would also be leading the creature there to finish off the job the monoliths had started. Jim pushed through the fog of fear to try to focus on the geologist and the path to the new dam.

It would mean leading the creature to more water, too. He decided it was a chance he had to take, and set off. He rode hard to keep his distance from Arvin, but frequently glanced in the mirror. He looked forward again just in time to see the car pulling out in front of him. He swerved. The car clipped his rear wheel and the world spun, then slammed into him, hard. He felt bones crack in his lower leg and his chest. The world turned gray.

"What in God's green earth were you thinking, boy? You could have gotten yourself ki—oh, that leg doesn't look good at all," an older female voice said. "I'll go call an ambulance."

"No, no time," Jim tried to tell her. "Dr. Miller…"

"Mr. Miller isn't a doctor, hun, he just collects rocks and such."

"Minerals…" Miller had corrected him so many times since he'd been helping out at the temporary lab, that it was his last thought as pain overwhelmed him and the world faded to a gray fog.

th to the new dam.

It would mean leading the creature to more water, too. He decided it was a chance he had to take, and set off. He rode hard to keep his distance from Arvin, but frequently glanced in the mirror. He looked forward again just in time to see the car pulling out in front of him. He swerved. The car clipped his rear wheel and the world spun, then slammed into him, hard. He felt bones crack in his lower leg and his chest. The world turned gray.

"What in God's green earth were you thinking, boy? You could have gotten yourself ki—oh, that leg doesn't look good at all," an older female voice said. "I'll go call an ambulance."

"No, no time," Jim tried to tell her. "Dr. Miller…"

"Mr. Miller isn't a doctor, hun, he just collects rocks and such."

It would mean leading the creature to more water, too. He decided it was a chance he had to take, and set off. He rode hard to keep his distance from Arvin, but frequently glanced in the mirror. He looked forward again just in time to see the car pulling out in front of him. He swerved. The car clipped his rear wheel and the world spun, then slammed into him, hard. He felt bones crack in his lower leg and his chest. The world turned gray.

"Minerals…" Miller had corrected him so many times since he'd been helping out at the temporary lab, that it was his last thought as pain overwhelmed him and the world faded to a gray fog.

***

"Wha? Where am I?" Jim woke, disoriented in a strange living room. His leg screamed with pain, while his ribs stabbed him with every breath.

"You're in my house, son. I'm Mrs. Swinson. You're lucky my Ricky was home. I'd have never been able to drag you across the street."

"Uh, thanks," Jim said. The windows rattled.

"Storm comin', good thing you're off the road on that motorbike. Never did like those things."

"No ma'am, not a… not a storm. Can't explain. Gotta get to the dam," Jim fought to talk.

"You're not goin' anywhere, bub. We called the police, and it's more'n we shoulda done for you, causin' an accident like that," Ricky said. Ricky Swinson. The name clicked for Jim now, a couple of years ahead of him in school, could have gone pro as a pitcher until he hurt his shoulder. Major jerk. Jim tried to get up, but even shifting his weight intensified the war of sensations coming from his lower leg. His stomach turned. He leaned back onto the couch.

"I guess you're right. Is my bike all right? Will it run?"

"It's pretty banged up, why?" Ricky asked. "You're not riding it anywhere with your leg all… whaddayacallit when it stick out? Competent fracture or somethin'?" Another tremor, audible this time, made the figurines on the mantel over the fireplace dance.

"Because that's not thunder. That's the reason I was going so fast and not lookin' too good where I was goin'. It's… It's too weird to explain. Were you in town last week?"

"During the storm? The flood? Nah, I read about it in the paper, but I was at college."

"It was no storm, I mean, sure there was rain at the end, but that's not what destroyed the geology office or the dam. They blew up the dam, on purpose."

"The devil you say." Another thump, bigger. A couple of figurines plunged from the mantel to the floor. One hit the carpet, one smashed on worn floorboards. Jim knew which ending he and the Swinsons would get if he couldn't convince Ricky to take the message to Miller.

"I swear it's true. Look, you got a pen and some paper? You take a message to Dr. Miller up at the dam. He'll know what to do."

"This is just ridiculous. We've still got phone service, unlike most of the town, and my cousin Annette is on switchboards today, so I know the operators are working. We can call from here," Mrs. Swinson offered. "We can clear this right up before the ambulance comes for you."

"Oh no… The ambulance, coming from town?" Jim said, eyes widening.

"Where else? You stupid or somethin'?" Ricky asked.

"You don't understand. If they're coming from town, they'll run right into him!" Exerting himself, Jim pushed back the curtain and looked down the road. A tiny black form like an army action figure stood out against the horizon, smoke billowing up behind it. "Too late, I don't think they're coming."

"What? Let me… what it heaven's name is that?" Ricky stood, staring out the window, one hand on the sill. The house shook again. More smiling porcelain figures shimmied to their dooms.

"That is a persistent storm, isn't it, Ricky? Why don't you take down the rest of my collection before the whole thing is ru—lord in heaven! Annette! Oh my, no Annette, listen. Forget about Mr. Dale's garden. I've got to talk to Mr. Miller. I'm told he's over at the dam office. Down? Any way you can get me the police station and they can radio up there? Yes, I'll wait, but hurry! It's—there's—I don't even know, just make the call! Get Chief Corey if you need to!" Mrs. Swinson was practically crying now, tapping her foot and shaking her free hand while peering out the window at the slowly growing figure in the distance.

"Annette, we don't have time for this, something… something's coming down the road. Tell Mr. Miller it's happen"You're in my house, son. I'm Mrs. Swinson. You're lucky my Ricky was home. I'd have never been able to drag you across the street."

"Uh, thanks," Jim said. The windows rattled.

"Storm comin', good thing you're off the road on that motorbike. Never did like those things."

ing again!" Mrs. Swinson slammed down the phone. "Pick him up, we're getting in the car," she said to her son. A minute later, Jim lay in the back seat of a sky blue Chevy Bel Air as Mrs. Swinson peeled out onto the road, headed for the dam.

Behind, the creature stomped onward. Jim pulled himself up briefly. Were there other, smaller figures at its heels? The ambulance drivers? At any rate, the forest of growing spires followed where Arvin went.

***

"What is that thing, anyway?" Ricky demanded. They turned onto Dam Rd. while he focused his mind to answer.

"It's—it *was*, my cousin, Arvin. I really don't know what happened. We were cleanin' up Dr. Miller's lab in town, stopped for lunch, fell asleep in the back of the truck. We worked hard this mornin' and it was so nice with the breeze and a full belly… When we woke up, he looked all funny, gray. His hand getting wet and… His hand! He cut himself in the—" The car slewed to the side as the impact of the massive stone feet on the hillside loosed the earth from its rest. Mrs. Swinson stomped the accelerator, sending up rooster tails of sand and gravel. The car's tail end spun clockwise until the tires gripped rock and they lurched forward, jostling Jim, graying the world again as his leg and chest released new waves of pain.

, now, but the road up the hillside was unpaved and winding. They'd kept ahead of Arvin by relying on the car's speed, but now they were slowed by the terrain. At the first switchback, Ricky looked out the side window.

"Floor, it ma! There's more of 'em!"

"I thought I saw more back at the house," Jim said, barely holding on to consciousness. "Gotta tell Miller…" Another footfall knocked rocks from overhangs. They tumbled down the hill, battering the car. The windshield cracked, then shattered as a chunk of dark gray rock the size of Jim's head landed in Ricky's lap. He gasped, holding his arm.

"I don't know what's goin' on, but he stopped 'em before, right?" Mrs. Swinson said, sounding panicked, "Dr. Miller?"

"What? What are you talking about? There was a flood. The paper didn't mention anything like this!" Ricky objected.

"Would *you* report hundred foot rocks growing in minutes, falling, and crushing things? Turning people to stone, too? It sounds like science fiction, the product of a deranged mind! I'd be afraid I'd be locked up in my own little rubber room fed meals by nice young men in their clean white coats… How bad is your arm?" Jim asked.

"I'll survive. It's barely bleeding. I'll have a bruise tomorrow. Stupid rocks." Ricky shoved the rock out the broken side window. More boulders slammed into the car from the side, sending it toward the cliff's edge. Thin blades of dark stone sliced through the car's body, sticking into the passenger compartment. Jim looked back again. The giants were waving their hands like they were throwing things. He ducked as another barrage came in, smashing the back window and stabbing into the seats.

Mrs. Swinson did her best to avoid the tumbling and thrown stones, driving closer to the brink, then zigging back toward the wall on the left. Jim marveled at her calm and focus. Another tremendous crash dropped tons of rock onto the road, burying the switchback and starting a rock slide that wiped away every trace of man's intervention on the environment behind them. For now, the giant and its cohorts were out of sight in the dust cloud. He they been buried? Was the danger over?

The Bel Air skidded to a stop on the new, deep black, macadam that still smelled of hot tar, ignoring the bright white lines and arrows denoting direction of travel. There were a handful of other cars there. Doc's Jeep was there among them. He'd made it up here and hadn't left yet. That was something. Grinding sound came from the roiling dust clouds that hid the slope toward the highway and seemingly, the rest of the world.

Ricky helped Jim out of the back seat and he stood with an arm over the older boy's shoulder.

"Oooeee, son, they really did a number on the ol' car!" Ricky exclaimed, observing the multitude of dents and dings, scratches, and knives of stone so thin as to be slightly translucent, making one side of the car look like a pin cushion.

"'Old'?" Mrs. Swinson objected. "This machine set our family back three thousand dollars not two years ago! It was meant to last for at least a decade! How are we going to get to the store now? Bicycles?" The woman huffed and sat on the hood of the car, staring out into the dust cloud, arms crossed.

The boys didn't have any answers, but had enough experience with adults to know there was no right thing to say. They merely peered off into the nothing as well, getting their breath back from the harrowing ride, hoping to see nothing. "That sound, it's just, you know… the landslide settling into a more stable position. All that loose rock. It's not going to just turn right back to solid ground like that," Ricky said, snapping his fingers. Could it be true? Had the problem more or less solved itself? They waited, listening intently.

"There," Jim said, "the rocks are shifting. That was definitely a footstep. We better keep on."

"I think you're right young man," Mrs. Swinson said, sliding off the hood and standing on her own again.

"Hey! You folks aren't supposed to be up here! This is a hard hat area!" An older man Jim didn't recognize yelled, waving a clipboard. Behind him, Jim saw Dr. Miller and some other men in hardhats coming down a ladder from a newly rebuilt section of dam. A trailer stood to one side, acting as the office during construction. A lone telephone pole stood halfway along the parking lot, bereft of wires, but guarded by a pair of portapotties in royal blue.

Just as Jim was about to answer the older man, a shriek like thousands of fingernails on blackboards tore through the canyon. Everyone squeezed their eyes shut and clapped their hands over their ears.

"What was that?" The man, now only a few feet away, said when the noise began to fade. The crash that shook the ground a moment later confirmed Jim's fears, but he still turned to look.

Ricky helped Jim out of the back seat and he stood with an arm over the older boy's shoulder.

"Oooeee, son, they really did a number on the ol' car!" Ricky exclaimed, observing the multitude of dents and dings, scratches, and knives of stone so thin as to be slightly translucent, making one side of the car look like a pin cushion.

"That!" He pointed with his free hand, still leaning into Ricky. Out from the rocks crawled a dozen dark gray figures twice the size of a person, lifting boulders aside with ease and freeing more crystalline giants. Beyond them, the trail of spires led back down the highway, past the Swindons' house to his own. He couldn't see the cliff from here, but the sheer number of monoliths brought despair to his heart. Would San Angelo survive?

Then Jim noted something altogether new, as far as he was aware. A pulse of red light slid along the stone forest toward them. As he watched, a yellow light appeared at the horizon, keeping pace with the red. A short time later, a blue light began snaking its way toward the dam, or perhaps, toward the giants who now climbed the slope.

"Holy Hannah!" Dr. Miller exclaimed on seeing the creatures.

"We're trapped!" Another of the men said. "That's the only way out of here, and road's just… gone."

"Hold onto your hat, Harry," Dr. Miller said, "Jim, what happened? The decontamination crew said the office was clear. Did you find the mineral somewhere else?"

"All I know is Arvin cut himself while we were picking up. It must have been a splinter of one of those rocks that changed him! I told him it was serious, that he should keep his mask on an all, but he wasn't around the other day when all this happened thee first time. He… I didn't make him understand."

"It's not your fault son. I should have stayed to supervise, and the clean up crew should have done a better job. That explains how he was exposed, but why the change in reaction? Did you see anything? Anything at all?"

"Uh, well… not at the office, but when we got back to my house and we were cleaning him up, we put peroxide on the cut, on account of germs and all."

"Mm hmm, wise, and?"

"I thought I saw something at the time, but I just chalked it up to being tired and hungry."

"What? What did you see?"

"When we put the peroxide on, you know, in the brown bottle," Dr. Miller nodded. "There was a little smoke that came off his finger, right where the bubbles were.

"Smoke… did the hydrogen peroxide somehow interact with these foreign chemicals? Causing them to change how they interact with the body? We may never know. I can't imagine anyone volunteering for such an experiment, or experimenting on animals with this material being condoned by the government… Thank you son. You did the right thing coming here to tell me. I'm just sorry that it seems like we're stuck here."

"What do we do now, doc?" One of the men asked.

"Salt water stopped these things the last round, but if it's propagating through a body instead of just pulling out the silicon from the sand and bedrock, it's running into quite a bit of salt and other contaminants. I'll need a sample of this new strain before I can even begin to come up with a solution," Miller said. "Let's all get back to the top of the dam and pull the ladder up after us. It's not much, but it will give us a bit more time."

"I second that! Maybe we can use the scaffolding to cross to the other side." One of the other men agreed and turned back the way he'd come. The others who had already been at the dam turned as well, but Miller held back.

"Can you make it, son?" He asked Jim.

"I think so. I don't know about the ladder with my bum leg, but I'll try. I did what I could to lead it away from town, to get to you. It's just not my day."

"You did the right thing, now let's get up there." Miller slapped him on the shoulder. A moment later, Ricky was leaning into Jim more than he was leaning on the larger boy.

"Ricky, are you o-? Oh no!" Jim tried to push himself away, but the other boy's grip was unbreakable, wrapped around his torso and pressing Jim's broken ribs into his hard chest. Black stars exploded in his vision.

"What's the—" Miller began to ask then cut himself off as he saw Ricky's face, dark and growing darker by the moment. The arm tucked around was Jim solid gray. Miller grabbed Jim's hand and pulled him free of the transforming boy.

"Ricky! No!" Mrs. Swinson cried, reaching for her son before one of the other men wrapped his arms around her waist and turned away, hustling as best he could for a dozen yards before putting her down and dragging her by the hand.

"There's nothing we can do now, ma'am. We've got to get away and keep ourselves safe long enough to find a means to defeat the invader's new form," Miller said.

"No! You healed the Simpson girl! I read about it in the paper! You found a way," Mrs. Swinson said, fighting to go back to her son. The throng of engineers and construction workers hung at the bottom of the ladder, wringing their hands and watching the edge of the hill. Before half of them were up to safety, gray heads wove into sight.

"That was with a lab and a medical doctor to consult. This is totally different," Miller said. One of the other men took up a mixing paddle from a trough of concrete and brandished it at Ricky to keep him at bay a few yards from the main group. Only a few small patches of flesh and clothing remained. The creature roared, swiping at the tool, spattering concrete all over itself and the ground.

It howled again, staggering backward. Steam hissed from where the concrete clung to it. The man swung the tool to fling more concrete on the monster, knocking it back further. "Look! I've got it on the run! Someone grab the other paddle!"

"You folks get up there if you can. Terry, Dan, help me mix up some more concrete. There's something in it that's reacting to the new mineral. Don't spill any pure water, though. If these things react anything like their predecessors, even a few gallons and any chance we have to contain them will be gone!" Miller instructed, making for the spigot where the hose was connected. The other men grabbed bags and began to tear them open.

Jim looked on, horrified that the boy he'd just met shared Arvin's fate. It must have happened when that gray rock landed in his lap while they were driving up the switchback to get to the dam. Jim cast a glance at the heads of the advancing giants, wondering which one was Arvin. He realized that many of them probably were, broken up and re-formed into humanoid monsters, just as the towers of the alien mineral had broken and multiplied, each fragment rising into a new monolith during the last crisis. Looking back at the men and Mrs. Swinson ascending the ladder, he was reminded of a siege on a castle.

"We should make a moat!" The thought popped out of his mouth as quickly as it arrived in his head, "Pour some concrete out in a line across the parking lot. They won't walk through it!"

"Great idea, Jim! Harry, grab a bucket and start slopping what he have out. A couple of feet wide should do it!" Miller pointed. The creatures had all crested the hill, now, and were stomping across the tarmac, three dozen figures ten feet tall, knocking cars out of the way and driving divots into the blacktop with every step.

While some men worked to cut off the creatures' progress and others went above to try to radio for help, Jim was stuck. With his ribs and leg busted up, he couldn't haul buckets or climb the ladder and there was no other way to the top of the dam. There was a backhoe, though. He'd learned to use one the summer before. If he could just get up into the seat and get it started, he could use the machine to push the monsters back and provide cover for the others. He knew Arvin wouldn't have wanted to hurt anyone, and

…if he could stop that, he would.

Reaching his arms out sent fire tearing through his chest. Ribs were definitely broken. He pushed through it, grabbing blindly for the bar to pull himself up. The next few minutes were

"You folks get up there if you can. Terry, Dan, help me mix up some more concrete. There's something in it that's reacting to the new mineral. Don't spill any pure water, though. If these things react anything like their predecessors, even a few gallons and any chance we have to contain them will be gone!" Miller instructed, making for the spigot where the hose was connected. The other men grabbed bags and began to tear them open.

Jim looked on, horrified that the boy he'd just met shared Arvin's fate. It must have happened when that gray rock landed in his lap while they were driving up the switchback to get to the dam. Jim cast a glance at the heads of the advancing giants, wondering which one was Arvin. He realized that many of them probably were, broken up and re-formed into humanoid monsters, just as the towers of the alien mineral had broken and multiplied, each fragment rising into a new monolith during the last crisis. Looking back at the men and Mrs. Swinson ascending the ladder, he was reminded of a siege on a castle.

"We should make a moat!" The thought popped out of his mouth as quickly as it arrived in his head, "Pour some concrete out in a line across the parking lot. They won't walk through it!"

"Great idea, Jim! Harry, grab a bucket and start slopping what he have out. A couple of feet wide should do it!" Miller pointed. The creatures had all crested the hill, now, and were stomping across the tarmac, three dozen figures ten feet tall, knocking cars out of the way and driving divots into the blacktop with every step.

While some men worked to cut off the creatures' progress and others went above to try to radio for help, Jim was stuck. With his ribs and leg busted up, he couldn't haul buckets or climb the ladder and there was no other way to the top of the dam. There was a backhoe, though. He'd learned to use one the summer before. If he could just get up into the seat and get it started, he could use the machine to push the monsters back and provide cover for the others. He knew Arvin wouldn't have wanted to hurt anyone, and if he could stop that, he would.

Reaching his arms out sent fire tearing through his chest. Ribs were definitely broken. He pushed through it, grabbing blindly for the bar to pull himself up. The next few minutes were Hell, with his leg and chest screaming at him in agony with every…

…heave, every stretch. Every breath was cut short, and sweat ran down his sides. Finally, he sat back in the bucket seat. Below, the construction workers had a decent moat begun, but the creatures were almost at the line they'd drawn on the tarmac. Would it deter them? He pushed the button to start the machine. It rumbled to life, shaking him, agitating his wounds. He gritted his teeth, pulled levers and stepped on pedals with his good foot.

Slowly, he edged the backhoe across the parking lot and stood guard over the men and their project. His idea. Was it a good one? Would it work? It was too late for anything else. He fought to stay conscious. One of the creatures got close. He nudged it back with the shovel. The next and next fell back, but the line of creatures grew thick. One made it past his swinging metal arm, stepping into the light gray mess, then another. Massive feet sizzled and smoked. Their owners fell back, bumping into others with a sound like a crate of glass bottles clinking. The creatures continued testing the barrier along its length.

At one side, the moat ran up to a sheer cliff face, up forty feet to the natural slope from which they'd blasted rock to create a space to work on the new dam… Blasting. He wondered briefly if there was an dynamite left, but then he thought of the shrapnel, and the army of creatures that would arise from such detonations. At the opposite end of the moat, another cliff, into the canyon along which the river had flowed for ages. Send them down into the water seemed inadvisable as well.

What else could they do? The concrete was clearly not going to hold them forever. Jim looked around and had another idea. He waved one of the other men up to take over on the machine and made his way to Dr. Miller. The man heard him out on the grounds of his earlier ideas and agreed. Miller passed out duties and they went to work setting up.

***

"We're out of concrete!" One of the men exclaimed, "The rest is already loaded in the mixer up there. We were going to pour before sundown. Should we turn it on 'em? Try to bury 'em?"

"They're kickin' up the tarmac, makin' bridges across the concrete. We gotta do somethin'!" Another man said.

"We *are* doing something!" Miller said sharply. "All we can do."

"How do we know it'll work?"

"It's got to."

Jim hung back by the ladder. He rested at the bottom of the wall, wondering what it was like to be a giant gray stone monster, if it hurt at all. He thought of Arvin and Ricky. No one ever thinks it can happen to them until…

The stone monsters crept along the parking lot, send up a symphony of chimes as they walked into stones from the rock fall and cars and each other. The men were ready, but would the plan work? Jim was out of breath with effort and fear, so he prayed silently. Using the crane that helped place the concrete forms, they grabbed one of the creatures and swung back over the dam. The metal claw opened, releasing the gray beast into the void between walls.

It fell, shrieking, and shattered on the rebar. The next few had the same reaction. It looked as though the plan would work. After the shards started filling the space, Miller signaled the team to start pouring the concrete. Hissing and sizzling abounded. Clouds of smoke rose up, wicked away by the evening wind. The sun lit the smoke as if the whole dam was afire. More giants fell, plunging into the pale gray soup, writhing for a moment, then settling .

Tiny creatures, spawned from the shards of the larger ones, formed rough heads, arms, legs, and moved toward the group of men still on the ground. The men pushed them away with concrete-covered paddles and knocked them into the mixing trough, which the claw grabbed and dumped when it was full.

Ricky!" One giant had a bit of white shirt showing on its back. Mrs. Swinson reached for him as he flailed through the air in the metal claw's grip. She fought hard, eventually breaking free of the men, only to trip a few feet from the edge just as the stone form fell into the fluid concrete. It flailed, hissed, smoked and screeched in an awful way that sounded too much like a wounded animal for Jim's comfort.

Mrs. Swinson knelt at the brink, swaying, staring down at the surface of the concrete. Jim felt bad for her, but had no idea what to say. He wondered what he would say to his aunt Maevis about Arvin. A few bubbles surfaced here and there, emitting more smoke which hovered like a ghost, white in the moonlight until the wind pulled it apart.

The sun had hung low in the sky when Jim and the Swindons had reached the dam. It had since slipped beneath the horizon, unremarked as work lights flickered on automatically. The valley below, and the desert plain beyond, were all cloaked in darkness.

Except… Except they weren't. The lights were still there, traveling on the path Jim suddenly thought of as the spine of a great serpent. What if…?

"Uh, hey doc, I don't want to, you know, make this day any worse than it already is, but what do you make of those lights?" Dr. Miller had been sitting on the steps up to the trailer with the other men gathered round, leaning on the stairs, the trailer, and in a few cases, each other, sunken to the ground and passed out from exhaustion.

"What do you mean, Jim? Show me." The pair ventured beyond the field of light the tall lamps provided, darkness enveloping them with a cool night breeze. Jim pointed.

"You see? Those colored lights running along the trail of monoliths? They don't seem to be growing right now, but that's the way we came, the way Arvin and his clones or whatever, chased us up here."

"This is something new. It will take time to study it and determine if it poses a threat. I don't want you to worry about them right now. As long as they're staying put, not collapsing on anyone or anything important, I think we can take a few hours to recover from the day. It looks like the giants didn't do much damage to the dam project, aside from the road. That's a blessing."

"I suppose, but I just watched two boys not much older than me get turned into monsters in one day, one of them my cousin, who I knew since I was born…" Dr. Miller laid a hand on Jim's shoulder.

"I understand that, but we can't dwell on these things. Remember the best times with these boys and hold onto those memories, maybe write them down in a journal. That's where I keep my most important memories. I've had to buy a whole new box of pens and two more notebooks in the last week to cover all the things I've lost but want to hold onto in my mind." Jim nodded. It seemed like sound advice, but the lights, the way the monoliths seemed… alive, still bothered him.

Dr. Miller stood with Jim for a few minutes, then said, "I think they're planning on rationing out the food from the coolers soon. It was just meant to be dinner for the workers, but we have to stretch it to you and me, and Mrs. Swindon, though she's so distraught, I don't know if she'll even take food. Tomorrow, we'll have to send someone down to the highway, to try to get into town, or at least somewhere there's a working phone. You'll have to stay here, with your leg…"

"Thanks for splinting it up. At least I can walk, a little, but I think you're right about getting back down this giant hill, let alone back to town… You go. I'll hobble along in a minute." Dr. Miller patter his shoulder again and retreated toward the light.

Jim stared at the lights. Where did the monoliths come from? Space, it seemed, but what if they were sent? The thought had crossed his mind before. But if some alien intelligence had sent them, what was there purpose? To clear the path for conquest like in some Saturday night double feature at the drive-in? To make the Earth inhabitable for their race? To communicate? If it was the latter, he didn't understand the message unless it was that the aliens were bullies and they could walk all over humanity. This thought riled him, and he picked up a chunk of broken macadam and hurled it as far as he could. The movement jarred his ribs and his leg, but it felt like fighting back.

As he searched for answers, he stared at the shifting lights. He almost felt like he could discern a pattern in them, a message. The monoliths weren't sent as a weapon, but an offering of peace. If his people could learn to understand them, use them properly, they would be able to improve their own lives, advance their technology, understand the world better, even go to space, to the moon. Yes, the senders of the monoliths lived there, beckoned to him. The moon itself rose over the horizon as he watched, and the lights of the monoliths became all the clearer. Insight flooded through his brain.

Jim turned to go back to the trailer when he noticed his leg didn't hurt anymore, but he had a pain on his hand. He turned it over and spotted a blot of pale, wet, concrete on his gray palm. He shook it off and continued on, waving at the men and Mrs. Swindon. He had so much to tell them, so much good news! It was going to be all right!

One of the men yelled, something he couldn't quite understand, and pointed at him. He tired to explain what he had seen, but the rest of the men stood up, grabbing the mixing paddles and swinging them at him. A spatter of concrete slashed across his chest and legs. He bellowed and stomped. How could they not understand him? He needed to get cleaned off. There was water there, that spigot.

Before he could reach the water, something grabbed him, lifting him high in the air. He spun, and saw the trail of glowing lights, so clear, so inviting, for a moment before he plummeted back down, striking the still-wet cement, sinking,

flailing,

smoking,

sinking,

burning,

sinking.

THE END??

JOHN A. McCOLLEY:

VICKIE SMALLS:

LUCIENNE LEBEAU:

Lucie... ...nce and guidance,
Michael ... the fun and fantastic

MICHAEL STRONG:

Michael ... the support and laughs, and the ... opportunities.

wp QUIGLEY:

Those who have come before:

Aaron Ara... ...Nick Holland, Chris Philbrook, Ha... Balizet, ... Black, Madi Quinn, Misha "DokTor Azathoth" Tuesday, and St... ...umphre... My only wish is that all receive the best of luck and good f... ...now tho... am grateful to each and all for your contributions and y... ...in... DOUBLE FEATURE and ASCENDENT PUBLISHING ... ...ay.

Those who are here in present:

Words do not accurately describe how grate... ...ored I am each and every day to interact and work with o... ...e projects we engage in. I appreciate you, I am humbled by you... ...in your service for as long as I am invited to d... ...K YOU!!!!!